THE
*S*CANDALOUS
*D*IARY OF
LILY LAYTON

THE
Sweetest
TABOO

THE
SCANDALOUS
DIARY OF
LILY LAYTON

THE
Sweetest
TABOO

STACY
REID

Entangled Publishing, LLC
2614 South Timberline Road
Suite 105, PMB 159
Fort Collins, CO 80525
rights@entangledpublishing.com

Scorched is an imprint of Entangled Publishing, LLC.

Edited by Alycia Tornetta
Cover design by EDH Graphics
Cover photography by PeriodImages

Manufactured in the United States of America

First Edition February 2019

entangled
scorched

For my love, Du'Sean. Because you said, "I do not love you because I had hoped you would give me children." And I believed you and we are still here today. I adore you.

Chapter One

The small, dark brown leather book appeared quite innocuous until one dared to fold back the worn cover and skim the first few pages. Oliver Simon Carlyle, the ninth Marquess of Ambrose, had been reading the same entry for the past several minutes, unable to credit the words written in such elegant, flowing script. Absolutely nothing at all indicated the lascivious and shockingly arousing content of what had revealed itself to be a diary of the most scandalous sort.

Dearest Diary,

My husband, God rest his soul, said my desires are abhorrent and unladylike and had admonished me most severely. I tried so hard to be proper, but it seems I am destined to be damned. Last evening, I stood in the eastern secret passage in Belgrave manor and watched as Lord R parted his lover's legs and licked her glistening slit. Lady W screamed, grabbed his head, and rocked onto his face. She appeared so wild and so wonderfully free.

To my utter shame and pleasure, I got wet, so achingly wet. I ran as quietly as possible through the hidden passage to my chamber and flung myself under the covers. God help me, I touched myself. I was not ladylike…I thrust two fingers deep into my slippery channel and—

Oliver closed the slim black leather volume softly, a harsh breath hissing through his lips. He had been reading the diary for the last hour, unable to stop, though he was consciously aware these were the private thoughts of someone who would never have shared such private and wanton feelings with him. Or anyone else, for that matter.

These were the deepest secrets of a lady attending his mother's week-long house party. The party had, in truth, been at his request, so that he could view a potential bride in an intimate setting instead of the more public marriage marts of the season. If Oliver recalled accurately, there were only fifty guests in attendance, and at least thirty were of the fairer sex. Now he was consumed with one question: who was the author?

The idea that a lady of the *ton*, even if she was a widow, had written such thoughts was positively indecent, and—since he was being honest—vastly intriguing and titillating to his jaded tastes.

With a rough scoff, he dropped the diary onto the stone bench on which he reposed. He would leave it where he'd found it, and possibly the owner would retrace her steps and recover it soon. Clearly, it had not been left to the elements and discovery for long. A light rain had fallen earlier in the morning, and the pages of the diary were dry...and arousing... and sinful.

Cursing himself virulently for his weakness, Oliver grabbed it and randomly picked a page.

Dearest Diary,

Sir Elliot offered for me today. I confess to being surprised, for though he paid calls upon me a few times, the baronet never expressed a romantic attachment of any sort. There is a distinct appeal to remarrying a man who already has his heir. I would once again be the mistress of my own home, and I would have the amiable companionship of Sir Elliot, without the expectation to produce issue, since he has his heir, a spare, and the most delightful little girl. If only he were not twice my age and more of a father figure to me. It is quite distressing to imagine running my tongue over his chest and down to his manhood as I had attempted with dear Robert. Perhaps Sir Elliot would be similarly disgusted with my wantonness and—

Oliver snapped the book closed and tilted his head to the sky. *Bloody hell.* She was young if she considered the baronet, who couldn't be a day over fifty years, old enough to be her father...and her dead husband had been called Robert. That should narrow down Oliver's search.

What the hell am I saying? He had no interest in discovering the identity of the author. To what purpose? He couldn't return her diary with any explanation that would not cause her great distress. Even if he lied and said he hadn't read the pages, her mortification would be great, indeed.

Nor could he leave it where he found it on the grass under

the cypress tree by the gazebo for another unsuspecting soul to stumble upon her lusty and scandalous musings.

Perhaps he should simply burn it.

He glanced toward where he'd found the damning journal, his gaze assessing each young lady who strolled by. None looked anxious, and a few gave him inviting smiles, no doubt hearing wedding bells, since it had been made known he was on the hunt for a wife. He was two and thirty and was quite bored. The usual debauchery that privileged gentlemen of his ilk enjoyed no longer seemed exciting. The pleasure gardens, the reckless racing, scandalous pursuits, and even the rousing debates in Parliament hardly moved him anymore.

There was an emptiness in his soul he couldn't understand, and nothing of late seemed to fill the void. He had bid his last mistress *adieu* over eight months past and been without a lover since. Oliver had seen no point in searching for another when his last three had left him so uninspired and frustrated. His mother had even clucked and urged him to take the waters in Bath to cure his ennui.

It was as if the world were painted in shades of gray, and he was waiting for a ray of something...*anything* to burst through the bleak dreariness and inspire him to simply feel.

One of his closest friends, the Duke of Basil, had taken the plunge into matrimony several months past, and the man seemed at peace and happy with his new duchess. The arrow of envy that had pierced his heart whenever he spied them together had stunned Oliver.

He had never begrudged a man more in his life. The duke had found love with Elizabeth Armstrong, an American heiress, and had shocked society. His Grace also seemed content and not likely to procure himself a mistress, which meant the duke's American satisfied his darker cravings. And Oliver had some notion of what they were; after all, they had both shared Lady Wimbledon for a night or two...at the same time.

Oliver wanted a similar happiness. In fact, he quite hungered for a wife...and eventually, children. That need was tempered by his keen desire to find a lady who would appreciate *all* his desires—even the ones a few of his mistresses had labeled as depraved and shocking. That had been his main reason for not rushing recklessly into matrimony.

His father had taught him at the age of sixteen that a wife must never be subjected to his base and darker urges. Mistresses were designed for rough and carnal tupping, and it was to be expected that he should have two women to sate all his needs.

Except...Oliver did not want that. He'd seen how it had torn up his mother and put a strain on his parents' marriage. But this was a notion that would have sent his father to an early grave, had he not already passed a few years ago.

Oliver stood, the book gripped lightly in his hand, and strolled down to the lakeside. The waters were blessedly empty, as most of the guests were playing croquet or already indulging in a light luncheon on the freshly mowed lawns. A few boats had been prepared for rowing, and he untied the ropes tethering one and climbed aboard. After securing the diary on the inside of his superfine jacket, he grabbed the oars and propelled himself farther out onto the lake. Once he was a safe distance from the shoreline, he stopped rowing and allowed the boat to drift at its own speed atop the placid waters.

Though he had decided to destroy the diary, he would first consume its pages. Interest had taken hold of his mind, and he wanted to read as much as possible, perhaps everything, before he chucked it away. He opened the slim volume once more and started to read. After a few minutes, a few truths made themselves evident.

The author was familiar with the inner workings of

Belgrave Manor and its secret passages. Perhaps she had visited before and not just for this weekend's house party. A friend of his mother?

Oliver's closest friend, Thomas Pennington, the Earl of Radbourne, had been in residence for a few weeks, and the little minx had sojourned in the secret passages of the east wing, which led to the guest chambers Thomas stayed in. Oliver was positive he was the Lord R referred to in her diary entry. Apparently, his friend had a mole on his left backside and a manhood that could have been more impressive. *Sweet Christ.*

A rough chuckle escaped Oliver. What would Thomas say if he knew one of Oliver's lady guests traversed the hidden hallways and spied on him while he had his pleasures? No doubt the earl would be amused and seek to uncover her identity so he could seduce her, too. Thomas was a notorious rake and libertine who enjoyed the challenge of a conquest far too much.

A swift denial roared through Oliver at the very idea. If anyone were to seduce his mysterious author, it would be him.

He paused as that awareness settled inside him. He was vaguely startled to feel the prickling of heat rushing through his veins, since there had been a distinct lack of interest on his part for any female companionship of late. Oliver delved into the pages, engrossed in her musings. He vacillated from anger to amusement.

Her husband had slapped her because of her unladylike desires, and the shame she expressed for having them made Oliver wish the man were alive so he could call him out and put a bullet through his priggish soul. What a blathering fool, to have been blessed with a woman of unrestrained passion, only to reprimand her harshly for what appeared to be her natural sensuality. Her husband had been a man like Oliver's father, who believed wives should display no cravings of the flesh—those were reserved for mistresses.

As he read further, a pattern in her artful words emerged. Each time his mother had hosted an event, the mysterious author had made use of the secret passages of his estate. The widow was, indeed, someone intimately familiar with his mother, for her to have been invited to the last two balls and the garden party last month.

His heart slammed hard inside when his name leaped from the pages.

Dearest Diary,

The Marchioness of Ambrose introduced me to her son a few months past at her garden party, and I do not believe he even glanced at my face. I, however, was inexplicably aware of him, in a manner I have never felt with another man. He hardly notices me, nor do I recall the marquess ever favoring me with his charming sensuality. But I notice him—the width of his shoulders and the power in his body. I've found no flaw in those wide shoulders, lean waist, and long limbs. Ambrose intrigues me. There is something lonely about his eyes, and those unsmiling lips have been haunting my dreams of late. What would it be like to be held, kissed, and taken by such a man? This inappropriate need I can feel stirring inside must stop. However, I am at a loss how to do so. No doubt the marchioness would be appalled if she had an inkling of the cravings her son has been inspiring inside me.

Oliver chuckled. *Sweet Mercy.* With one entry, his interest multiplied infinitely. What he would do if he discovered her— or what he would say—eluded him, but now it seemed as if his entire existence hinged on meeting her. His mouth went dry, and anticipation scythed through his heart, the eager feeling making him falter.

He was not a reckless man, nor was he the sort to be controlled by his desires. If that had been the situation, he would have been haunting the darkest and most decadent brothels in London to purchase women to sate his rougher cravings. His friends had never understood the desire he had for a lover…someone with whom he had more of a connection than simply riding them to fulfillment and never seeing them again.

He'd tried it once, had traveled to Soho Square and visited London's premier brothel and pleasure palace—*Aphrodite*. After several hours of debauchery, he had been wrung dry and his cock had hung limply, but inside there had been the echo of emptiness and unfulfillment that had lingered for months. He hadn't repeated the experience, to his friends' dismay.

Find her…

The temptation whispered in his mind and arrowed down to his cock. Oliver scrubbed a hand over his face, unable to accept that he wanted to act with such recklessness. For it was certainly foolhardy to be so consumed with trying to find the author. Where in God's name would he even begin? The secret passages spanned both wings of Belgrave Manor, but from what he could tell, she only seemed familiar with the eastern one. What could he do? Haunt the corridors of his house simply to uncover her identity? And then what… seduce her?

If his mistresses had been unable to accommodate his needs, he doubted a genteel, respectable lady would be willing to indulge them without hysterics.

What if she is the one?

He tumbled the idea through his thoughts. Without a doubt, she was a lady of society, young and seemingly willing to remarry. She wasn't a virginal debutante who would be prone to hysterics the first time he pushed his cock between her lips and farther down to massage the back of her throat. A groan escaped as the image blared through his mind. Frustration surged as the shadowy figure bent on her knees sucking his cock drifted away like smoke in the wind. He wanted her face, her hair...it was this unknown woman he wanted to picture.

He glanced down at the diary clutched in his hands. He would probably regret the impulse, but he would find her. She was here in his home, perhaps traversing the secret hallways. Oliver had to start acting now. The house party would be over in seven days, and then she would vanish. He tucked the book inside his jacket, grabbed the oars, and pushed himself to the shore.

A few moments later Oliver strolled across the lawns toward the side entrance. A few short minutes later, he entered his manor.

"My lord," Branson, the manor's at times pompous butler, intoned.

Oliver handed him his jacket and top hat. "Where is the marchioness?"

"Her ladyship is in the Rose room, my lord."

Oliver ambled down the hallway, bypassing the library for a smaller and more intimate drawing room his mother favored. After a perfunctory knock, he pushed open the door and entered. His mother was seated by the windows, knitting, and the only other occupant was her lady's companion, Mrs. Layton.

His mother glanced up and, warmth lit in her hazel eyes. "Oliver, what a marvelous surprise. I thought you would have been in Town until Friday. I know you deplore house parties, and I believed you'd only be coming down for the ball. I'm quite pleased to see you are dedicated to the pursuit of a wife."

"Mother," he greeted her, bending low to press a brief kiss on her cheek. "I thought it prudent to be here as early as possible."

She beamed in approval. His mother had wanted him to find a wife and fill the nursery ever since he reached his majority. Over the last few years, she had been encouraging him to make his choice, more like a thorn in his side than a loving matron. He'd made her the happiest mother in society when he had announced his intention to settle down.

There was a rustle, and he glanced around in time to see her lady's companion chewing furiously to get rid of whatever edible she had consumed. The lady quickly washed down the remains with a few healthy swallows of her tea. After setting the cup back in its saucer, she launched to her feet.

"My lord," she said a bit breathlessly, dipping into an elegant curtsy.

The dark blue muslin dress she wore seemed a bit tight, and her breasts strained delightfully at the top. He snapped his eyes upward, appalled at the direction his thoughts had taken. This was the second time he'd had an inappropriate thought about his mother's companion. The first had been a month ago, when he had come upon her on her knees in this very room, trying to reach for a button under the chaise. Her rounded ass had been temptation itself, and a visceral image of sinking his cock into her while she was in that very delectable position had blasted through his mind.

He had blamed his reaction on the fact he had been without a woman for several months. Oliver had suppressed the chaotic urges in his body and had departed without a word. He had never been the type of man to seduce servants or dependents in his own household. No, that had been his father, who had tupped every chambermaid he could get his hands on, humiliating Oliver's mother without regard for her honor and sensibilities.

"Mrs. Layton," he said, a bit too icily, for in her widened eyes he spied confusion at his terseness. Directing his attention back to his mother, he asked, "Have you compiled the list of eligible ladies?"

"Oh, Oliver, I am so pleased you are taking such interest. Mrs. Layton and I were just discussing the best candidates," she said, plucking a sheaf of paper from the small table and handing it to him.

More likely his mother had been chatting constantly, and Mrs. Layton had politely listened with that fascinating expression she wore of genuine interest and sympathy. He was glad his mother had hired her. She had been somewhat melancholy of late and had seemed to be sinking further away. He had encouraged her to be out more in society and hadn't protested when she informed him the late Vicar Layton's widow would take up residence at Belgrave Manor. Mrs. Layton had been an unexpected surprise. She seemed to be witty and charming and, to his mother's delight, engaged her quite artfully on various topics. The last discussion he had overheard was on the mating habits of rabbits.

His lips twitched at the recollection. "I will leave you ladies to your needlework and peruse this list at leisure in the library."

"Wonderful," his mother said with a wide smile. "Dinner will be at eight. I will arrange for Lady Victoria to be seated beside you. The earl's daughter is quite a delight and a very accomplished painter. I thought that would give you something to talk about, given your common interest."

He dipped his head in farewell then spun on his heel. As he neared the door he faltered, an awareness teasing his consciousness. He glanced back at Mrs. Layton, who had been watching him depart. She flushed but curiously did not look away.

"You are out of mourning, Mrs. Layton." He was used to

her in widow's weeds. Black or dark gray had been her choice for the six months she had been within his household.

"I… Yes, it has been two years."

Inexplicably, he lingered over her features. There was something else different about her. Ah…her hair. No longer did she wear the odious white cap that normally hid her hair. He'd seen wisps peeking from beneath the cap, but never could Oliver have imagined the glorious beauty she had suppressed.

She had the darkest, wine-colored red hair he had ever seen. God's blood.

She graced him with a tentative smile. He stared at her mouth, unable to take his eyes off her sensual lips. By some thoroughly irritating twist of fate, his mother had hired the one woman he found himself unwillingly attracted to. A dependent in his home. And the undoubtedly prudish widow of a vicar. The lady would possibly descend into hysterics and quit his mother's service had she any notion of the thoughts she inspired.

Biting back a savage curse, he gritted his teeth and left the drawing room before he said something foolish. Oliver made his way to the library and went over to the side mantel, where he poured a generous splash of brandy into a glass. He took several swallows then sat in the chair closest to the fire. There were fifteen names on his mother's list of eligible young ladies he could consider for courtship. A few he was familiar with from last season.

A name leaped from the page. Lady Penelope Dodge. Oliver had once spied her in a compromising situation with one of his closest friends, the Earl of Bainbridge. It had been a masquerade ball last season. Oliver had concealed himself in the library when Bainbridge had entered with the young lady. He had been caught in a quandary, for to reveal himself would have caused the young lady great embarrassment and possibly started a scandal. So, he'd sat in the dark and listened as his friend coaxed Lady Penelope to her knees to suck his cock. From the dim light of the fireplace, Oliver had watched her innocent hunger as she'd taken the earl in her mouth and had felt that jerk in his gut for a similar pleasure.

Bainbridge had taken her that night on the carpeted floor, and Oliver had watched her deflowering, sipping his brandy. He knew his friend had made an offer for Lady Penelope's hand a few days later, but he was rejected by the lady herself when society became aware of the precarious state of his finances. Many doors had been closed to the earl once it was discovered he did not have money even that of obtaining a wife. It seemed her loss of virtue had been inconsequential, for a husband without wealth wasn't to be tolerated.

Oliver mentally struck her from the list. Not because she was no longer pure, but because he had no interest in a marriage that at the foundation was only a business transaction—and, not inconsequentially, because Bainbridge was still in love with her. Oliver assessed the list, appreciating the selections his mother made. The rest of the ladies were all from fine families, with suitable dowries, impeccable bloodlines, and without any stain or scandal attached to their names. It was a great pity there was no indication of the young ladies' characters. He wanted the opposite of what his parents had—there should be no cold silence at his dinner table, no stilted dances at balls, no weeping when he visited his wife's bedchambers.

In fact, there would be no appointments to bed his marchioness, as many lords arranged. He wanted passion, the more spontaneous, the better, and they would be sharing a bedchamber. With his wife, they would have rousing debates and engage in inconsequential discourse. They would be playful and attentive with their children. He would make love with her, but he would also take her raw when his mood demanded it, and she would be with him every step of the way.

He closed his eyes with a sigh of defeat. He was setting himself up for profound disappointment. Could such a woman truly exist?

Perhaps not, but he would start his search with the authoress of the diary.

Tonight, he would step into the secret passages to encounter disappointment...or temptation.

Chapter Two

The marquess had noticed something about her. The shock at the very idea of a man so self-assured, powerful, and sensually appealing deigning to notice her did not ease the panic churning in her stomach, tempting her to cast up her breakfast of eggs, ham, and toast. Lily Layton held her smile in place through sheer willpower. The Dowager Marchioness of Ambrose prattled on, completely oblivious to the turmoil Lily currently endured.

Her diary was missing.

Her thoughts raced, trying to remember if there was anything within its pages to identify her as the authoress. She'd been careful to leave no trace of her identity as she poured out the improper cravings in her body and soul onto paper. But how could she have been so careless as to not realize it had slipped from her basket when she'd taken her morning stroll? Lily blamed it on the shocking news she had received prior to indulging in her early walk. Lady Ambrose no longer desired Lily to continue as her lady's companion.

Several months after the death of her second husband,

the local vicar, the marchioness had imperiously ordered Lily to move into Belgrave Manor and attend to her. The vicar had been a puritanical, social-climbing despot who had done everything to ingratiate himself with Lady Ambrose. The marchioness had tolerated his reverent obsequiousness, and she had been incredibly kind and courteous to Lily. She'd accepted the position of companion to the marchioness, for her widow's portion had been only one hundred pounds, and the cottage she had resided in with Robert was needed for the new vicar.

Lily had staunchly insisted that the position must be a paid one, though she was quite aware of the graciousness of Lady Ambrose. She'd had nowhere to go. Her parents could not afford for her to return home to their small cottage and be an added burden to their already strained resources.

Lady Ambrose, bless her heart, had acceded to Lily's exorbitant request for three guineas a month for her services. She had been saving whatever she could, but she had not put away enough to ensure a future for herself that would not rely on her choosing another husband. The last thing she wanted to do was marry for the third time, especially if another husband required children.

Familiar pain and grief welled in her heart, and she had to push it away before the tide of despair could suck her under.

"It is time, my dear Mrs. Layton, for you to secure your future."

Lily lowered the teapot carefully onto the beautifully designed French rococo table. "I am not sure I comprehend your meaning, your ladyship," she said with a small smile that felt too tight. Though the marchioness meant well, Lily did not appreciate her future being decided by anyone but herself.

"Come now, surely you wondered why I no longer require your companionship. You are delightful, to be certain, but it would be selfish of me to keep you to myself when you need to set up your nursery with another husband. I've recently found an unmatched happiness with Lord Clayton," she said, blushing prettily and patting her elegantly arranged coiffure.

Viscount Clayton had been paying particular attention to the marchioness, and Lily had suspected they were lovers. Lady Ambrose tended to blush whenever she met his gaze, and, once, she had even seen the viscount sneaking from her bedchamber at dawn. Lily had been quite happy the melancholia that had weighed the marchioness down seemed to be melting away. She was still a very beautiful lady, with only a few streaks of gray in her dark hair and some soft wrinkles on her face. Her beauty was ageless, and Lily was pleased when the sparkle had returned to her hazel eyes.

She did feel a pinch of pain at being discarded so easily, but she brushed it aside. It was not as if she had planned to reside at the manor for the rest of her life. She had hoped to stay only until she had saved enough to open her shop in London and had made a few notable connections through the marchioness.

It seemed like an impossible dream on most days, becoming a premier modiste with a shop on Bond Street or Cavendish Square or even High Holborn. She would specialize in riding habits and rival even the most notable dressmakers with her unique and elegant creations.

"My lady, it is kind of you to think of me, but I am quite happy here at Belgrave manor with you."

"You need a husband to help you manage, my dear. It's the way of the world."

Lily barely resisted scoffing. "That, I assure you, Lady Ambrose, is the last thing I require. I do not need a husband to supervise my life and restrict my dreams and passions. I'm five and twenty. I quite believe I am capable."

A twinkle appeared in the marchioness's eyes. "My

dear, there are those husbands who happily allow their wives freedom."

"I am more interested in safeguarding my future using my skills and intellect, my lady. Husbands do not last forever, and I may marry a third time and find myself widowed again, with my future unsecured."

"Pish!" The marchioness waved aside her protest. "I've seen the longing on your face when you think I am not looking. I've already hired another companion, and Miss Julia Waverly will be here by the month's end. I will host our local ball early this year, and you will find a suitable gentleman from the village. You are young, with very pretty eyes and lovely smile. It will not do for you to waste away here."

"Thank you, your ladyship, but—"

"I'll not hear your objection," the marchioness said with a harrumph. "I've seen the looks you've been casting at my son."

Dear God in Heaven.

Lily could only stare at Lady Ambrose, frozen in indecision. "You are quite mistaken, my lady. I cannot imagine a more ludicrous notion. If you have seen me staring, I assure you, I have only been admiring the cut of his jacket or studying the richness of the material. You know I am forever fascinated with fashion, and I am quite determined to be a sought-after modiste of the *ton*."

The marchioness could have no idea that Lily's dreams had been filled with the marquess doing wicked things to her body with those firm and sensual lips. She had never acted inappropriately within his presence. In fact, the man hardly acknowledged her. It was as if he did not see her, so faded was Lily into the background of their lavish lifestyle. She was simply the hired help with the lovely euphemism of lady's companion.

The marchioness pinned her with a searching glance, her

lips pursed in a moue of disapproval. "You must come to the ball on Friday, my dear," she said, giving a benevolent wave of her hand.

A ball! A shimmer of excitement went through her. "My lady—"

"Sir Ellington is in attendance, and I've detected the keen regard he pays to you. Mr. Crauford also seems decidedly interested. He is the grandnephew of Baron Hayford, so Mr. Crauford is not without connections, and he commands two thousand pounds a year. My dear, I don't believe you will be able to secure better."

"Oh, no, my lady. The offer is most kind of you, but I must politely decline."

"Nonsense. If you are worried about your wardrobe, I have the most delightful gown that with only a few alterations will fit you quite well. If you are a seamstress worth her salt, two days should be sufficient to make the changes to your satisfaction."

Lily stood and strolled to the window overlooking the lake. She did not like the fierce burn of excitement that had flared through her. She had never been to a prestigious ball before—only several country routs, which had been immensely delightful.

"Your ladyship, I appreciate the kind offer, but I truly have no desire to attend a fashionable ball." *Liar*, her heart cried softly. It was vastly appealing, but what would be the point? She did not belong to that extravagant world.

"Every young lady wishes to attend one of my balls," the marchioness rejoined, with an arrogant lift of her chin. "If you have any hopes of capturing Mr. Crauford's attention, Friday's ball will see it done. When he sees how you comport yourself within high society, he will be more apt to court you, despite you having no dowry or suitable connections."

There was little point in reminding the marchioness that

she did not desire marriage. She had already endured two, and despite the saying, the third time would not be charming, pleasant, or amiable, but a reoccurrence of banality and shame at her wanton heart. However, Lily could not ignore the opportunity that attending the ball presented. This could be her chance to impress the ladies of high society with her designs. She could alter the gown in several ways, ensuring she outshone many there, and perhaps they would be compelled to ask after her dressmaker. That was the way to foster the connections of which she had been dreaming.

"Thank you, your ladyship. I believe I will accept your offer of the ball gown."

The marchioness nodded approvingly. "Wonderful, Mrs. Layton. The dress is from last season, and I only wore it once, for I did not find the color flattering. The soft rose would look quite charming on you, my dear."

She rang the bell, and a maid hurried in shortly after. The marchioness ordered the gown to be delivered to Lily's room and also for a picnic hamper to be prepared.

Lily smiled. "Do you need me for the rest of the morning, my lady?"

"You may have the rest of the day." She cleared her throat, her cheeks flushing pink. "Lord Clayton and I will be having a light repast in the south gardens before joining in the outdoor games."

Lily dipped into a quick curtsy and departed, belatedly realizing the marchioness had required her presence less of late. Their afternoon readings had been canceled for more than a week now, and their last weekly jaunt into the village had occurred almost two months ago. She faltered, pressing a hand to her stomach. How had she not noticed? Because of her inattentiveness, she had less than a month to plan for her unencumbered future.

She pushed open the door and collided with Lady

Lucinda, the marquess's younger sister, a petite, blue-eyed brunette with slender curves, a winsome smile, and a most charming personality.

"Oh, dear me!"

Lily smiled. "Lady Lucinda, how are you today?"

Her eyes twinkled, and Lily had the sneaking suspicion the girl had been eavesdropping.

"Dear Mrs. Layton, may I prevail upon you for assistance?"

"In regard to…?"

A generous smile curved the girl's lips as she considered Lily with an odd sort of anxious scrutiny. "I need you briefly in the music room. I am trying to practice my steps for the waltz, but Mr. Potter doesn't seem inclined to indulge me today."

Lucinda waited expectantly, and Lily stared at her for several seconds, embarrassed but delighted at the girl's kindness. "You are very thoughtful, Lady Lucinda, but it is very unlikely I will be asked to dance at the ball. And you should not eavesdrop."

Lucinda flushed. She had a romantic soul and was quite naive in the matters of the heart, and Lily loathed the day the girl would realize marriage was not all that she imagined it to be. Lady Luciana was eager for her debut and had spoken of little else for the past few weeks.

"Please, Mrs. Layton, indulge me. It will also help me prepare for when I am launched into society. I want to be as graceful as a swan when my *beaux* twirl me about the floor. And you just may be asked to dance. Imagine how mortified you would be if you had to decline because you are unable to."

Lily smiled at her earnestness. "I've been persuaded, but not now. Perhaps in a few hours."

Her entire face lit with her smile. "How glorious. You

will not regret it!"

"You are welcome, and I thank you for thinking of me," Lily said, smiling. She hurried to her room to collect her bonnet. She would also select a book from the library so that, under the pretext of reading outdoors, she could surreptitiously search for her diary. That was all she would direct her attention to now, for she could not imagine the ghastly effect of her personal reflections falling into someone's clasp, especially if they discovered that Mrs. Lily Layton, widow of their beloved vicar, was the author of such sinful thoughts.

Several hours later, Lily stared at the ceiling of her bedchamber, unable to settle. Worry had wrested her slumber away, and she feared it would not return. She had retraced her steps several times, and there had been no sign of her diary on the lawns, the sitting benches, or on any table or mantel anywhere. She had even searched the library shelves and tables in the event someone had mistaken it for a book and thought to return it. There was nowhere else to look, and she hated the tight band of anxiety across her chest and the tears forming behind her eyes.

Once again, she tried to calm her racing thoughts and recall everywhere she had been. Suddenly, she stiffened and slowly sat up on the bed as something came to her. Early this morning, she had taken a walk through the secret passages before attending to the marchioness. Sometimes the darkness of those hallways was a haven hidden away, where she could breathe and allow herself to be wicked in her imagination. That was also the place where she had, quite by accident, come upon the open portal that gave her a direct view of Lord Radbourne's guest chamber.

She pushed from the bed, relief and hope rushing through her veins. Perhaps it had fallen out of her basket there. Though she suspected a secret panel led to her bedchamber, she hadn't located its entry despite her numerous searches. But there was one she could enter through in the library. She slipped from her room, comfortable with the dark, almost running in her haste, down the long hallway and then the stairs, her voluminous cotton nightgown wrapping around her legs.

A few moments later, she paused at the library door and stood still, allowing her senses to detect if there was another presence within. Confident the house was asleep, she gently opened the door. There was a fire burning low in the grate, but the room was blessedly empty. Lily closed the door behind her and hurried over to the bookcase. Shifting several books on the third shelf in the far-right corner, the bookcase moved and revealed the beginnings of a dark staircase. Lily grabbed a candlestick from the mantel, lit it from the fire, and proceeded into the passageway.

The bookcase closed behind her, the draft of wind almost putting out her lone candle. The flames flickered but then held firm. With a soft sigh, she turned left, moving toward the east wing where most of the guests resided. After several minutes of searching, the hollow feeling of despair surfaced once more. Her diary was not on the floor of these hidden corridors.

A loud moan had her faltering. Lifting the candle high and looking around carefully, she blushed at realizing she was once again standing by the portal in front of Lord Radbourne's chamber. There was a thump, what sounded like a giggle, then a lusty cry.

She closed her eyes, denying the urge to spy on the earl and his lover. The first time she had heard the sounds, she had opened the small wooden panel, not certain what she would find, for she had never imagined that bed sport elicited such lustful cries. Her shock had been profound when she'd found the earl's mouth buried against Lady Wimbledon's snatch. Lily's sensibilities had been distressed, aroused, and she'd been rooted to the spot, unable to pull away from the intimate display.

A discordant sound rode the air, and she stiffened. She frowned, listening. There it was again. She strained to hear, and Lily almost fainted as footsteps sounded along the passage of the secret corridor where she stood. She inhaled sharply, clutching the candlestick tighter.

Someone was coming.

The awareness settled like heavy stones against her chest, crushing and frightening. How could she explain being in the passage that allowed her a scandalous peek into the earl's bedchamber? Dear God, why had she given into the wanton urgings and sinful temptations of her heart?

The footsteps grew closer, but she stood frozen in indecision. If she hurried away, whoever it was would hear her scampering and perhaps rush after her. The candlestick slipped from her nerveless fingers with a *thunk* onto the floor. She held her breath, sure the earl and his lover had heard. Thankfully, the light was out, so she pressed against the wall, hoping she had not been seen and the person in the dark with her would walk by, leaving her unnoticed.

"Ah...we meet at last," a rough, low voice drawled, distressingly close.

A moan of denial and shock hissed from her.

Dear God, I've been discovered.

"I never really thought I would encounter anyone...but here you truly are," the voice continued, the merest hint of amusement and perhaps intrigue coloring his tone. "Have I shocked you speechless?"

He had poleaxed her senses, for he intimated he had

expected to find someone here. In all her months of exploring these dark, secretive corners, she had never encountered another soul. The fact that he had arrived without a candlestick hinted of his familiarity with the winding passages.

"Who are you?" she demanded, her voice husky from apprehension.

"A kindred spirit."

"I hardly believe that to be possible." He stood just a few feet away, and she had to look up to where his voice came from. Even in the blackness, she could tell he was tall.

"Permit me to ask your name," he said smoothly.

"A jester, I see." As if she would ever be silly enough to reveal her identity. She had pitched her voice low to disguise it. She wondered if he'd done the same.

"I've never been accused of being overly humorous before."

She clenched her hands into a fist. "No, I will not provide my name."

He chuckled. "Ah, you would prefer anonymity."

"I would *prefer* for you to let me pass unmolested."

There was a pause. "I do not prevent you, my lady," he said with a heavy tinge of regret. "You are free to leave."

Yet her feet did not move, and she remained pressed against the walls, ignoring the chill of the stone. Who in God's name was in the dark with her and why was she lingering in his presence? He could ruin her reputation. Though she hadn't consented to remarry, she hadn't fully given up on the notion. She sometimes wished for a companion, a friend, a lover, and a happy home, but she wanted it with a man who would not make her ashamed of her sensuality and wanton cravings, and a man who would not terribly mind that she could not produce issue. If ever there could be such a man.

"Or you could stay...and we could just *be*," he murmured, his voice low and rough with something dark and all too enticing.

His emphasis had her mouth drying. That dangerous, forbidden thrill shot through her again. The very one that had caused her late husband to slap her across the cheek and call her a whore on their wedding night.

He's gone, the temptress lurking inside whispered.

"Who are you? No—" Lily hurriedly amended. "No names, please. Do you know who I am?"

There was a moment of tension. "No."

Her eyes widened in disbelief. "Truly?"

"Yes." His voice rang with sincerity.

"Do you wish to know?" Not that she would ever tell him, but she was beyond curious as to his presence.

"Only if you wish to tell me more. I know you're a widow."

"I beg your pardon?" How could he know such a thing? Did he suspect her identity and only toy with her? Anger at the notion seared Lily, and anxiety burned inside her.

"There are no young ladies present in the manor who would dare to be so bold to tour these dark hallways. That would be quite extraordinary, wouldn't you say?" There was an odd vein of amusement in his tone.

"What else do you know?" The question was harsh.

"Relax," he urged. "I know you're a lady, without a doubt one of Lady Ambrose's guests. But which one?"

Some of the tension leaked from her. She wasn't a lady, and if he thought it so, it would be much harder to decipher her identity.

"I will not insist on more until you are ready to tell me."

Which she would never be. "You are in no position to insist on anything." An untrue statement, for he had all the power in this exchange. He could easily overpower her and drag her to the library.

"I will cajole politely, then."

There was that hint of provoking amusement again.

She thought about that for several seconds. "What do you want?"

There was a low chuckle of anticipation that made her shiver. Good heavens.

What does he want?

Her heart jerked. Could it be that he wanted to spy on the earl as well? Shameful heat scorched her body, and she was absurdly grateful for the cool darkness. "Why are you here?"

"I read your diary."

For precious seconds, she couldn't breathe. "I beg your pardon?"

The very air around them went remarkably still.

"I found your diary...and read it. That's how I knew where to find you." His voice was as dark as she imagined sin would be incarnate.

Her heart was a tattoo against her breastbone, and she could only stare in the direction of his voice at a complete loss. Then fury rushed through her. "Those were private thoughts! You, sir, are no gentleman," she snapped, being very careful to keep her voice low and disguised.

"Ah."

There was a wealth of meaning in that single word.

"I regret the discomfort I've caused you, but I do not believe I can proffer an apology, for without reading your diary, I would never have found you. I had the thought that perhaps there was a woman with whom I could experience the things I've long wanted to do with a lady."

She bit into the softness of her lips, desperately wanting to ask what things. She should be running from this situation, even if there was a risk of revealing her identity when she spilled from the secret chamber into the lighted library.

"Your restraint is admirable," he said, his voice roughened with provoking amusement. "I'm fairly hopping on my toes to tell you my desires."

The dratted man was a still menacing figure of darkness before her.

"Perhaps I do not care."

"Are you the author of the diary...or an unwitting reader like myself?"

Apprehension skittered across her nerve endings and mashed painfully with the arousal writhing through her body. *Lie*, a voice inside warned. "Why is that important?"

"That author would desperately want to know all my lewd fantasies—she is fearless with her desires."

Oh, the way Lily had always wanted to be with her hidden thoughts, fearless and free. Surely this man was not a gentleman of society? Gentlemen expected ladylike demureness from their wives. Who was he to possesses such an unrestrained mind? "You do not think her, the author of the diary you found, a whore?"

"No," he clipped icily.

"That is unusual," she said softly. "And what...frightful desires do you possess?"

"Are we to have a frank conversation, then, my lady?"

"I'm—" She caught her slip just in time. It was so instinctive for her to refute that she was a lady whenever someone granted her the honorific in error. The sneaky scoundrel. He did want to know her identity. "We are, my lord."

A pulse of silence, then he made a low groan of appreciation.

The sound of a consistent slapping and thumping reached them, and Lily flushed in mortification when she realized it was the earl and his lover, and the thumps were of the headboard against the wall.

A guttural moan issued from the earl as his lover begged for more, some shocking demands spilling from her lips. Lily's breathing roughened. She was afraid and aroused beyond measure.

She sensed when he moved closer.

"Ah, Lady W and Lord R."

Her knees weakened. How mortifying, he had read *that* particular entry.

"Do you like watching?"

She blushed, grateful the darkness hid her reaction. What must he truly think of her? "To ask such a private question is not the mark of a gentleman."

"Why don't we leave all expectations of gentlemanlike and ladylike conduct…in the library."

Blast her irrepressible heart for being so captivated by the scandalous notion.

"Do you like watching?" he repeated.

"*Sir*, I—"

"We are strangers in the darkness," he murmured. "There are no rules here."

The breath left her lungs. "I…"

"Don't speak, just look."

Her heart jerked, but she stood still, trying to understand the weakness assailing her and the growing persistent throb in her core.

"Allow me," the stranger murmured, the warm heat of him brushing her body.

He shifted the small portal, and as if the chaotic cravings controlled her, Lily slowly turned toward the opening.

The earl was between his lover's spread legs, and his mouth was pressed against her feminine channel.

The man behind her stepped closer. "Tell me, why do you like watching?"

Embarrassment assailed her, and Lily clenched her hands into tight fists. "I don't—"

"Let's not quibble, my lady. I know you do…I could tell from your journal. You've walked these halls, and you have watched Lord R and Lady W. You stumbled upon them once…and you went to your room and pleasured yourself with your fingers…didn't you?"

Dear God. Her heart stuttered in the most painful rhythm, and Lily drew in a trembling breath. "Yes."

"Since then, you haven't watched them…why not?"

"I…" She had felt confused, embarrassed, and too needy. "My mortification overwhelmed me."

His fingertips danced over the nape of her neck, and a tingling shot straight down below her navel. Her entire being focused on that single sensation.

"There is no need to feel shamed by the need to watch… to see the myriad of expressions on her face as her cunt is ravished. There is a voyeur in all of us, from the maiden who wishes a glimpse of a bare-chested man to the gentleman who desires to see the delicate flash of a lady's ankle, the shadow between her succulent cleavage, the flash of curls covering her most intimate parts. We all hunger for a taste of something forbidden, only some of us have the audacity or courage to act on those needs."

Lily couldn't fight the awakening of the wanton part of her soul. The temptress inside lifted her head and reveled in his sensual assurance. "An inexplicable longing filled me when I saw Lord R and Lady W, one I could not overcome. I lacked the courage to keep watching, certain I would be taken over by a desire that could never be assuaged."

His fingers skimmed across her hips lightly, and instead of pulling away, she leaned into his bold and improper touch. A rough sigh of appreciation dragged from his throat. Lily understood. Her acceptance of this stranger's touch meant she was open to scandalous pursuits, which had been his intention to discover.

The touch of his hands on her hips burned through her nightgown. She had never been so conscious of another before.

"The earl and his lover would have reveled in the knowledge that you watch them."

That notion was positively indecent...and thrilling. "How do you know?"

She felt his smile against her shoulder.

"The earl and I have shared Lady W...and I know their carnal desires."

Lily gasped.

"Tell me," her mysterious stranger coaxed. "I want to know your cravings."

Lily knew without a hint of any doubt that her life would never be the same if she succumbed to the lust in her heart. But she didn't want to return to that realm of uncertainty, of restraining of one's passion and true heart.

"I enjoy seeing Lady W's expressions of pleasure. Sometimes I do not know if she writhes in pain...or delight. I love the nuances I see on her face, I revel in the cries that spill from her throat, and I ache when I see her come undone for the earl. I want to be her. I want to feel such bliss...and I want to be splayed wide and taken while others watch me." The confession felt as if it was wrenched from the hidden recesses of her soul, where she had interred her most depraved urgings. She closed her eyes tightly, bracing for some manner of repudiation.

Instead...a hum of approval echoed in the dark.

Lily's entire body weakened, washing with heat at the feel of him against her back.

"Are you watching?"

She snapped her eyes open and wetted her lips. "Yes." Her voice sounded hoarse and so unlike her, Lily didn't have to work hard to disguise her tone.

They watched together in silence as the earl adored his lover in the most carnal manner Lily had ever seen. "Do you do that?" She almost fainted as the words spilled unbidden from her.

"Do what?"

"What the earl is doing."

"Licking his lover's quim?"

His wicked words erotically stroked her senses. "Yes," Lily whispered.

"Most assuredly," replied the stranger.

His roughened voice made her ache for things that often left her blushing when she thought about them. Her heart picked up its rhythm as temptation and impossible desires beat at her. How many nights had she lain awake dreaming of passion and wicked deeds?

You harlot.

No, the woman inside her roared at the ghost of her husband's voice. *No more.*

"Do not try to find out who I am."

"I swear it on my honor," came the stranger's immediate reply.

"And I do not want to know who you are."

"As you wish."

A sigh of longing pulsed from her. "I want...I want..." Words failed her.

"Tell me."

She couldn't speak through the tight knot in her throat. He waited, and she distantly admired his patience. Lily closed the portal, shutting away the image of the earl twisting his lover to sit atop him. She wanted to ask about every scandalous thing she had wondered but had been told was too shocking for a lady to know...even a wife. "What is the most improper and unladylike word you know for what happens between a man and woman...when they are in bed being intimate?"

"Tupping, swiving, prigging...but my personal favorite is

fucking."

Oh. Thick anticipatory silence blanketed them. She could not bring herself to say her shameful needs.

"There is freedom in the darkness. Say what you want. Take what you want." His voice was a whisper of velvet across her skin.

Freedom in the darkness. He was the devil. This stranger was the only man to ever ask what *she* wanted. He was in a position of power, he could simply take her if he wanted, and no one would be the wiser.

The darkness whispered around her, safe and sheltering, yet also electrifying and dangerous. "I want...I want your mouth on me *there*," she whispered, stepping off the edge of recklessness into the freedom her heart had been hungering for.

Chapter Three

The words lingered in the darkness...an offer for this stranger to sweep her away. The awareness of the depth of trust she placed in him was frightening. She was giving him her body, unreservedly. But better yet, she would be able to be gloriously wanton without being reprimanded.

"You want me to lick your slit."

She couldn't fight the need that thrummed through her body. Years of pent up arousal, of hard-won control shattered in that instance. "Yes."

A soft hiss slipped from him, but she heard it. She felt bold, adventurous.

Serious, reserved Lily was gone, and in her place was the woman she had always longed to be. She was a temptress...a wanton, or perhaps simply a woman indulging in mutual pleasure for the very first time. Well, she hoped pleasure would be mutual...he seemed knowledgeable of the sensual arts.

She felt when he dipped, and then a soft kiss was pressed on her shoulders, felt the warm caress of his breath against her throat. Trepidation and excitement melded into an indistinguishable whole. He pushed her nightgown up to her waist, baring her bottom to the cool draft in the hidden passage. Lily's breath rasped from her, and she trembled. She was allowing a stranger to touch her with such shocking familiarity. He bunched her dress in front of her and pressed her closer to the wooden panel. A large hand, smooth, without calluses, settled with firm possession on her hip.

A gentleman. Not the hand of a worker, or a servant. One of his fingers tapped her mound, sending little vibrations to her clitoris, which rested below that taunting finger.

"How long since your husband passed?"

"Long enough." *Two years and three months.*

"Have you had lovers since?"

He addled her thoughts. "How is this of import?"

He ran his fingers down to her already damp slit. His action was so unexpected, she jolted at the contact.

"I simply wondered how hard I could take your pussy without worrying about your sensibilities."

Her mind blanked, then a startling rush of pleasure burned through her, and liquid soaked his fingers. Her cheeks flamed.

His chuckle was low and heated. "You know what I mean when I say pussy."

"Yes."

"How?"

"I...I've read a few books. *Memoirs of a Woman of Pleasure* and others."

"Ah, the depraved delights of *Fanny Hill.* Were you shamed for reading them?"

She closed her eyes tightly against the memories. "No one knew," she whispered. "But I felt ashamed for what they made me *crave.*"

"Did you study any of the erotic drawings?"

"Yes."

He brushed his lips against the side of her neck, and she tilted her head to allow him better access.

"What if I told you after I lick and suck your cunt… your quim…your velvet tip, I want to tup you. Do you know whereof I speak?"

"No," she said hoarsely, though she had some idea from the dark, lascivious way he whispered.

He turned her gently, and her unreasonable heart wished she could discern his features.

Unexpectedly, he cupped her most intimate area. "This is your pussy…your quim…your cunt. If you want me to be polite…your pleasure garden, your velvet sheath."

Lily moaned, barely able to breathe. "I don't want polite."

His hands stroked upward, tugging her nightgown down to her elbows, baring her breasts to the chill in the passage. Her nipples beaded instantly. His palms molded themselves to the full mounds of her breasts, his thumbs and forefingers capturing her peaked nipples and rolling them.

Sweet mercy.

The sensations filling her were like nothing she could have imagined. He arched her, and his tongue stroked over the sensitive tip of her nipple. A hungry moan broke from her throat as he repeated the caress. She pressed against him, gasping for breath as his lips sucked at her breast.

He dipped two of his fingers into her mouth, and she curled her tongue around them and sucked. Then he pulled them from her lips and traveled down to her core.

"Open for me."

Her body hummed with nerves and anticipation. She complied. There was no tenderness. No caution. Just a dominant touch. She was wet, warm, slippery, inviting this stranger to caress her. Using his thumbs, he carefully parted and spread her feminine folds to rub his fingers over her sensitive nub.

They drew a shaky breath together.

"Open wider," he commanded.

Dear lord, she spread her legs even farther and invited him. He stooped and lifted one of her legs over his muscled shoulder. "Brace your hands against my shoulders," he growled.

She instinctively obeyed.

He cupped her buttocks in both his palms, tugged her forward, and pressed her core to his mouth. Lily cried out, and one of his hands shot up to smother the weak, breathless sound she made. Her body shuddered at the domineering clasp over her mouth, and the feel of the long slow licks that parted her feminine folds to delve deep inside her. What they were doing was so very wrong but in all the right ways.

He held her under the wicked lash of his tongue, and with each lick and nibble, this stranger devastated Lily's sensibilities. He gripped her buttocks firmer, angling her closer to the stroke of his tongue. She whimpered, helpless to stop the lustful sounds spilling from her throat. Being so vulnerable and intimate with a stranger went beyond her most desperate and lustful dreams. His teeth settled over her pleasure spot, and he gently nipped, then sucked, intensifying the excruciating sensations already destroying her mind. She bit down on the flesh of his palm in a desperate bid to prevent her scream.

She had never felt anything this good, not even in her tentative exploration of that little nub. Agonizing pleasure seared through her body, and with a muffled cry against his palm while fisting his hair, she unraveled.

He stood, breathing harshly.

"I'm going to take you." Despite his rough assurance, she heard the question in his voice.

"Yes." The fulfillment she would feel when he entered

her was enough to make her breath catch with need.

He nudged her legs wider, gripped her hips, and lifted her. She gasped at his strength, for she was not slender, but too rounded, as her last husband often lamented. Her mysterious lover settled her on his thick thigh with an ease she found even more arousing. Lily clasped his shoulders, anchoring herself, for her feet were barely touching the ground.

His hands brushed against her stomach as he undid the flaps of his breeches. Was he nervous? Were his hands shaking like hers? His fingers whispered over her clitoris, nearly throwing her into another climax. A large hand cupped her cheeks with surprising tenderness and pulled her lips to his. *Oh!* The taste of herself on his lips was strange... but arousing.

Lily moaned softly and parted her lips to his questing tongue. How strange... She had never been kissed with such intimacy before. It was as if he savored and consumed her in equal measure. His tongue stroked her, licking her teeth, her lips. Lily gasped into the embrace, her senses shocked.

He worked his hand between them and settled his thumb on her nub of pleasure.

"You're delightfully wet," he groaned.

"I can't help it."

A hum of approval sounded, and the striking pressure against her clitoris increased with a few rough glides. She whimpered as his ministrations grew in intensity. Three fingers dipped inside her slit, opening her wider than she'd ever been before. She gasped at the unexpected stretch.

"My lady," he said, his voice raspy, "bury your face in my neck and bite down on my shoulder if you feel the urge to scream."

She did as he commanded. He pulled from her, and a hard, blunt pressure nudged her entrance. The hot, swollen tip of his arousal pressed against her. There was a feeling of charged anticipation, a flash of heat, and then he thrust, parting her unused muscles, which clung too tightly, resisting his possession.

Lily climaxed with a muffled wail on that first deep stroke. *Oh, dear God.*

"Tight," he said, the word more a grunt than anything else.

He withdrew, the drag of his thickness forcing shivering delight through her. Her lover plunged back into her, hard and sure.

"Ugh," she moaned. The pleasure-pain was a burning sensation that started where they connected and spread to her throbbing clitoris. It hurt, but deliciously so.

He rubbed her nub with quick firm strokes, filling the sensitive bundle of nerves with pained bliss. A whimper tore from her, and she bit into the soft of his neck. It was his turn to groan his appreciation.

"Can your pussy take more?"

Her entire body blushed at his crudeness, but her wanton heart purred.

"Yes...no...*I don't know*," she sobbed, but her hips arched into him, demanding what her lips wouldn't.

He gradually withdrew from her, and her flesh resisted, the snug fit making her core ache. His hands gripped her hips even tighter, easing from her with excruciating slowness and then shoving back in. Lily wailed, mortified at the wanton sound that spilled from her. Despite the shock of being stretched open so completely, arousal burned through her body.

"Remember, you mustn't make a sound." The rough carnal drawl at her ears made her wetter.

She burrowed her lips even closer to his neck. Some unknown instincts urged her to part her lips and suck at the corded muscles of his throat. She did...and dear heavens, he glided from her and thrust deep and hard. Dark, wanton heat spread through her, and Lily found herself dropping one of her hands from his shoulder to grip his buttock. She squeezed, moaning in appreciation of the grind and flex of muscle as he surged inside her.

"I want more," she whispered.

"Easy...this first time we'll go easy. I promise after I ride you four or five times, I'll break in your pussy for the kind of wanton fucking you're craving."

"Oh God," she whispered breathlessly, unbearably aroused by his vulgar tongue, but startled at his assurance this tryst was more than one night. Lily hadn't thought beyond this moment. She nipped his ear, then laved the sting with her tongue. "I'm not a delicate flower, I can take more... *now*," she purred. "My...my cunt can take more."

His grip tightened, and he groaned, then hardened even more inside her.

"You *like* my vulgar tongue," she whispered, awed and aroused by his reaction. Lily gasped when he hoisted her and walked with her still sheathed on his cock in the dark. Surprise scythed through her when he pulled from her, dropped her legs, and tugged her down...to the ground. There were several rustles, and then he eased her until she was lying on her back. From the slide of material beneath her, she surmised she was resting on his jacket. The ground was chilly and quite uncomfortable, but she did not care.

A hand gripped her thigh and splayed her open, then his large frame blanketed her body. His cock surged inside her, and his satisfied grunt and her cry of pleasure echoed in the dark. He started to ride her, with long, deep strokes, filling her with bliss and taking away the bleak emptiness that had lingered inside for so long.

Her legs lifted, her ankles locking at the small of his back as she arched closer.

She clutched his shoulders helplessly and buried her face in the curve of his neck as he thrust into her clenching core with almost mindless fervor. Everything inside her collapsed and concentrated on the hard, almost brutal thrusts of his cock into her wet slit. Lily never imagined pleasure could be this sharp and all-consuming, and the fact that she did not know this man heightened her arousal to a blistering degree.

He worked her soaked sex until she trembled and sobbed and twisted her fingers through the thick strands of his hair, and her lover did not relent. A heavy ache coiled low in her stomach, drawing tighter as the piercing sensations intensified. She lifted into his thrust, her thighs falling open wider. She couldn't halt the scream that came from her throat as pleasure swept through her in a hot, unrelenting rush. Lily trembled, the muscles of her pussy clamping down on his cock until he could barely move. He groaned and shoved inside her repeatedly with such strength her buttocks slid against the cold ground.

She would be bruised later, but she could only concentrate on the shock of sensations ripping through her body. He took possession of her lips in a soul-destroying kiss as he found his own pleasure, pulling from her and splaying his warm seed atop her quivering mound.

Lily's senses were overwhelmed, and inexplicably, she felt like crying. Tears sprang to her eyes, and she tried to swallow past the lump forming in her throat. She searched the dark and could barely discern the outline of the man poised above her. His weight supported on his elbows, her stranger lowered his forehead to hers. His heaving chest rasped against her tender nipples, and she bit back a whimper. Everywhere ached, and she hardly knew what to do with herself.

This had been a fierce burn of insanity that was over too soon.

Her legs slid weakly from his hips, her arms falling to her

sides.

"Are you well?" She fancied his eyes glowed with tender emotions.

Yes... No. She had no notion of how to reply. What was there to say? This midnight encounter had rewritten everything she knew about herself. She wanted nothing more than to flee to the sanctuary of her bedchamber, to flee from this forbidden scene and the heart of the woman that had been revealed within her.

• • •

Oliver could feel the warmth of her breath on his face. Her elusive fragrance of honeysuckle and the scent of their combined arousal filled the air. He could feel the jerking rhythm of her heartbeat against his chest, and she seemed unable to respond to his concerned query. He frowned. Had he hurt her? She had been very tight, and he had been rough in his demands.

"Did I hurt you?" *Please God, let her say no.* The memory of one of his mistresses crying prettily into his handkerchief after he had taken her mouth with his cock roiled through him like a bad ale. The shock of that encounter had kept him from her bed, even though she had pleaded for him to return.

Why in God's name hadn't he tempered his passions more?

"You didn't hurt me," she said, her voice low and husky.

Thank Christ.

He eased away from her, barely able to make out the white of the nightgown in the dark. He had fucked her without any care for her sensibilities. Oliver scrubbed a hand over his face, never feeling so uncertain about anything in his entire life.

"Let me clean you," he murmured, reaching for his

handkerchief before biting back a curse. She was still sprawled on his jacket, her breathing choppy, and the silk he needed was in the pocket.

He drew her gently to her feet, holding her as she swayed in his grip. He barely discerned her motions as she tugged her gown over her breasts.

"I must go."

"Stay."

A sharp inhalation of shock.

"I meant, I understand," he said, ruthlessly tempering his responses. He didn't want to alarm her unduly. "Allow me to escort—"

"No!"

He belatedly recalled her request that her identity be kept secret. From her untutored responses, he did not believe assignations like this were common to the lady. It was as if he could feel her mortification, and he knew without a doubt she was blushing furiously.

"I...thank you for tonight. It was wonderful," she said softly, the pleased astonishment in her tone soothing the jangle in his heart.

"You've never climaxed before."

There was the slightest hesitation, then she replied, "No...I never knew. I must go."

"It will haunt me to not know who you are, my lady."

"I see years of torment in your future, my lord."

His lips twitched at her disgruntled retort.

"Please do not follow me."

"I swear on my honor."

He felt when she drifted away, her footfall a silent testimony of her familiarity with his secret passage. *Who are you?* After waiting for several beats, he made his way to the library. She had left the panel partially open, and he pushed it forward and stepped into the room. An elusive whisper of honeysuckle was redolent on the air. Of course, the library was empty. Still, a pang of disappointment pierced him.

Moving to the sideboard, he grabbed a decanter and poured a generous splash of brandy into a glass. He swallowed down the liquor, the smooth burn welcoming.

He'd been studying a few businesses that he wanted to purchase for weeks now, taking apart the finances and assessing if making an investment would be profitable. It had always amused his set that working on reviving flagging businesses, the more complicated, the better, gave Oliver a thrill that nothing could rival—except tupping a woman who was passionate enough to take him how he wanted...sinful and filthy on most days. He'd planned to work for the rest of the night, and he was mystified that he was undeniably stuck on what had just occurred.

He could still taste her sweet, musky tartness on his tongue...and feel her tight pussy ghosting over his cock. With this unknown lover, he hadn't even scratched the surface of the sexual needs that haunted him, yet there was a deep satisfaction lingering in his gut.

He drew in a hard, deep breath. Would she even venture into the secret passages again?

A knock sounded before the door was pushed open to reveal Lord Radbourne.

"You are decidedly disheveled," he said, closing the door and heading to the decanter of spirits.

"And how was Lady Wimbledon?" Oliver asked, ignoring his friend's dig at his appearance.

The earl grinned and licked his lips. "Delicious. I dare say my feelings should be bruised, for the lady keeps hinting at a desire to have both of us between her soft thighs again, and soon."

Oliver frowned as no response stirred within him. "I am not enticed."

"Come, man. Anna's charms are delightful." Radbourne paused in the act of drinking and slowly lowered his glass. "You are really not interested." His tone suggested how ridiculous he found the notion.

"I'm not."

"Is it your bloody investments? Or are you painting?"

"Neither." Though he wanted nothing more than to climb the stairs to his studio and immerse himself in the dark, provocative images that leaped to life on his canvas whenever he sought to quiet his thoughts. Frequently, it was if a madness seized him, and he would lose himself for hours—days, perhaps—while he painted, pouring his emotions into swirling colors of oil paint until provoking images of raw sensuality emerged. Rarely did he produce a tranquil picture.

"Ah, then it's this blasted rumor I've heard of you wanting to marry and fill your nursery."

Oliver merely smiled in reply and tipped his glass to his mouth, swallowing some brandy.

"Good God, man, say it isn't so," Radbourne demanded, appearing aghast and a bit shocked.

"It is so," Oliver said firmly. "Pray do not bother wasting my time with protests. I am decided. I need…no, I want a wife."

"Why in God's name would you desire the old ball and shackle?"

Radbourne had been declared one of the most profligate rakes of society and had been running from the parson's mousetrap for as long as Oliver had known him. The earl believed marriage for love to be a ridiculous notion. In truth, he seemed to disdain the institution of marriage altogether. Oliver had never uncovered the reason from his tightlipped friend and had been shocked when he'd declared his cousin would be his heir.

"Have you ever felt something is missing in your life,

Radbourne?"

The earl considered him for a few seconds. "No."

"I hunger for something more. And I know I will find it with a suitable companion."

"You are indecently wealthy, powerful, and healthy. What more could you want to be content?"

Oliver smiled. "Someone to love."

"Do not tell me you still believe that blathering nonsense about not keeping a mistress after you've wed. Upon my word, man, that is one woman to tup until death does part you and your marchioness."

"I'll not dishonor my wife. Only a dishonorable bounder would break vows made before his woman and God."

The earl scowled. "You forget I know your sexuality. We've taken women together, Ambrose. What gentlewoman will allow herself to be debased so? You are not thinking straight. Every man has a mistress; it is natural."

Was he being foolish in his desires? Oliver recalled hovering at his mother's door, listening to her sob to her maid of how his father had shamed her when he took her to bed. He remembered the guilt on his father's face that night as he drank several tumblers of brandy. It was then his father had reaffirmed his lessons, his voice rough with regret. His father's instructions had been explicit—when Oliver took a wife, he must never strip her naked, he should always protect her modesty and delicate sensibilities under the banner of darkness, he must never ask of her any unnatural coupling. Those requests must only be done with whores... or mistresses.

He had a duty to his family and bloodline and knew he would one day take a wife to fulfill that obligation. Oliver had never dreamed that his sense of duty would have translated that to the need for a companion, a friend, a lover, a wife he could adore and be adored by in return.

"What I want is not impossible. Basil and his duchess are blissfully happy."

His friend sobered and lifted his glass toward Oliver. "I wish you the best of luck…and when you find it, be sure to let me in on the secret."

"I will," Oliver promised, suppressing the insidious thought that he might be deluding himself and would never find that which he sought.

Or worse, it might just be another fleeting passion to chase, which would eventually fade, once more returning him to that world painted in shades of gray.

Except, not long ago, though wrapped in the arms of darkness, pleasure had been like a kaleidoscope of burning colors.

I must know who my secret lover is.

Oliver stared into the flickering fireplace, wondering if his mysterious lady would ever forgive him when he uncovered her identity. He had sworn on his honor that he wouldn't, but how could he allow her to slip through his fingers without truly exploring who she was? And it was the pleasures and the privilege she had granted him that made him want to know her, even though the tight grip of her sheath on his cock was the sweetest torture he had ever endured.

She could be a credible candidate for his wife. He already knew she could meet his needs on a physical and the most elemental level. Even if she were not able to handle all his desires, he would have a wife that was lustful, adventurous, and not overly worried about sensibilities.

What was she like? Bold, brave, quick with her repartee, that much he was certain. He needed to know more. Despite the evidence suggesting they had perfect sexual compatibility, he wouldn't marry a woman on such a meager basis alone. He was probably a damn fool, for many in the *ton* married with no true attachment in their hearts. But he wanted more than just an enthusiastic bed partner. He wanted a friend, someone with whom he could share matters of the estates or discuss the debates he had within Parliament, with whom he could take long walks and simply enjoy their marriage.

He didn't covet beauty, and he could tell even in the dark her curves were ample and delightful. But was she kind? Thoughtful of others beyond her desires? Would she make a suitable marchioness? What were her connections? How in God's name could he discover her identity and assess if she would make him an appropriate wife?

I don't yet know how...but I will find you.

Chapter Four

Lily had been sitting on the chair in front of her dressing table for at least half an hour. As a companion to Lady Ambrose, Lily had a room only a few doors from the marchioness. Her ladyship had rung her bell, quite demandingly a few times, but Lily had been unable to respond. It appeared the marchioness had forgotten today was her off day. And Lily was also finding it challenging to exit her room, knowing she may encounter her midnight lover in one of the guests.

I've lost all the good sense I possessed.

How could she have allowed a stranger inside her body… and she hadn't just invited him, she had been another person with him, wild and wanton…a *whore*. Her behavior had been ill-judged and beyond the pale.

Her throat tightened, and she leaned forward, studying her face in the mirror. Would anyone know she had been debauched? Her lips were red and kiss-swollen. Other than that, she could find no visible signs that she had been thoroughly ravished. Last night, she had fled to her room as if the devil had been on her heels, where she had tidied to the best of her ability with the small pitcher of water by her bedside. Lily had blushed furiously as she cleaned away his seed from her body.

Her hand had lingered across her stomach, and unable to suppress the emotions tearing through her heart, she had wept. Failing to conceive in two marriages had been a blow she was still recovering from. On most days, Lily mourned that she would never have a child in her arms, a daughter with her inquisitiveness, or a sweet boy who reminded her of Papa's generosity of spirit and quaint handsomeness. Pursuing her passion to be a stellar seamstress sometimes buried the pain, and she quite looked forward to the day when the ache of loss wouldn't be so sharp.

Her stomach rumbled, reminding her she had missed breakfast. With a sigh, she pinched her cheeks, hoping to bring some color to her face. *Who are you?* she mouthed silently and then felt silly when the pale woman staring back at her did not burst into speech. Lily was grateful it would not be evident that she had been altered on such a profound level. She shifted, and the tender, well-used flesh between her thighs ached. If not for that tenderness, she would have thought it another of her fevered fantasies. But it was all too real. She had been wanton with a man in a dark, secret passage. A horrified giggle slipped from her, and she slapped a hand over her mouth.

Who was the lustful creature that had possessed her body last night? Who was the woman who had *begged* to be tupped harder? And who was the man who had fulfilled years of pent-up longings?

"Oh God, who is he?"

It was an unrelenting desire to know who was in possession of her diary and her most passionate yearnings. Who was it that had made her unravel so powerfully? She had been exactly as her last husband had described her, a harlot, and he must have been correct in his assessment, for he'd possessed the ear of God. She had married a clergyman because he had been so sweet and amiable. Lily had felt tender sentiments toward him and believed what they had would grow to love. It had not, and she had felt bereft, adrift without a companion she could truly be herself with.

She waited for shame to wrap her in its arms, but no such emotion swelled within her heart. Lily smiled. How delightful to not feel guilty of something so carnal and wonderful.

A knock sounded, and the maid assigned to the marchioness entered. "Mrs. Layton, her ladyship has been ringing for you. I told her I would check if you were in your room."

Lily stood, smoothing her palms over her dress, though it was wrinkle free. "Thank you, Mary, I shall be right there."

"She is in the large drawing room, Mrs. Layton," the maid said with a quick bob, before disappearing down the corridor.

Taking an even breath and trying to find a reasonable excuse as to why she had been unavailable, Lily collected her walking basket from where she'd placed it on the small sofa by the fireplace. She hurried from the room and down the hallway then the winding stairs. She desperately needed to fortify her nerves. Perhaps she could steal into the library for a splash of the marquess's brandy.

No, she mustn't keep her ladyship waiting. Lily approached the drawing room and took a steady breath before entering through a door that stood slightly ajar. She faltered when she spied Mr. Barnabas Crauford, the man whom Lady Ambrose was encouraging Lily to take as her third husband.

The man's face lit up with genuine pleasure at seeing her, and she suppressed her groan. This was the last thing she needed now, the trouble of fending off his unwanted attention.

"My lady," Lily greeted with a quick curtsy, then turning to the dreaded suitor, she dipped into another curtsy. "Mr. Crauford."

"Mrs. Layton, how delightful you appear this morning." His eyes roamed her body in appreciation, and she was almost regretful she had abandoned her mourning garb and mobcap.

She wore a dress she had made and knew she looked quite fetching. She had needed to bolster her confidence after last night's farce and had adorned a dark yellow morning dress with a cinched high waistline that was very flattering to her figure. It was out of character, though, and she noticed Lady Ambrose considering her with a peculiar frown. Lily had also left her hair uncovered, catching it in an artful chignon while leaving several tendrils loose.

"You do look very pretty, my dear," the marchioness said, smiling. "I'm sure you will be delighted to take a turn on the estate grounds with Mr. Crauford."

"Of course, of course," he heartily agreed.

"I'd planned on visiting my parents. Today is my off day." She lifted her traveling basket for their perusal.

"I would be most obliged to take you in my coach, Mrs. Layton," Mr. Crauford declared.

Swallowing her sigh, she glanced out the windows. "I'd planned on walking."

Startled shock bloomed on his face. "To the village?"

"Yes, I find long strolls help me to clear my head, and I do so enjoy it."

"Capital! Allow me to at least keep your company part way."

He appeared so earnest that a smile tugged at her lips. She would be rude to reject him once more. "Thank you, Mr. Crauford."

The marchioness beamed her approval, and in short order, they departed the manor and headed south toward the beaten track that cut across the marquess's land. They ambled for a few minutes, and unable to endure another cleared throat from Mr. Crauford, Lily was prompted to speak.

"It is very kind of you to walk with me thus far. There is no need for you to continue."

"My dear Mrs. Layton," he said, a bit too warmly. "I would not be much of a gentleman if I abandoned you to the elements."

"I've been traipsing this path by myself for at least five years, Mr. Crauford. There is certainly no need to worry about my sturdiness."

"I am appalled the vicar allowed it."

She faltered momentarily. "My husband did not disapprove of my weekly visit to the village to see my family. And if he had, I assure you I would still have seen them."

"Upon my word, surely you would not have disobeyed him?"

Gripping her basket, she forged ahead. "In that regard, yes."

Mr. Crauford huffed disapprovingly, and Lily smiled, uncaring of what he thought. They rounded the corner.

"Look out," he yelled, shoving her aside with too much strength.

Lily gasped and tumbled into the bushes as thunderous hooves darted past. Surely it was only the grace of God that prevented them from being trampled by Lord Ambrose's stallion. Shocking and profane curses spilled from the marquess as he dragged on his reins, bringing the animal to a shuddering halt. Still, Mr. Crauford's act of chivalry saw her backside firmly planted on the ground and the contents of her basket spilled. "Blast it!"

"Are you hurt?" the marquess demanded, vaulting from his horse and rushing to her side.

For a wild moment, his concern warmed her before she

recalled he was the reason she was sprawled inelegantly amongst the bushes.

"Are you afflicted? You were rounding the corner far too fast. If Mr. Crauford hadn't been quick thinking, we could have both been under your horse."

Lord Ambrose's left brow rose at her audacious reprimand. "You exaggerate. I had control of my steed. He was simply overanxious."

"Mrs. Layton," Mr. Crauford said, tugging her attention to where he was gathering the contents of her basket. "This is not a proper book for a woman to read," he said picking up her copy of *Northanger Abbey*, which she had planned to read later while her parents slept. She had bought a couple of candles and had wrapped and stowed them carefully away. It was a relief they had not been damaged.

A severe frown split his brows. "This is unacceptable."

"Is that so?" she asked frostily, struggling to her feet and attempting to bat away the marquess's hand as he helped. The dratted man would have none of it, and with a gentle clasp, assisted her upright. "Thank you," she muttered grudgingly.

"Forgive me for startling you."

Sincerity glowed from his dark blue eyes, and that warm sensation once more unfurled in her stomach. The man was very handsome with his lean but powerfully built physique. Lily stepped away, desperate to create more space between them, hating that she was so ardently admiring his handsomeness.

"Forgiven," she said with a firm nod. "Please continue your ride." Then she hurried over to Mr. Crauford and collected her basket. After ensuring her sketchpad and her book were safely stowed, she assessed her clothes.

"I must say, your father has been derelict in taking you in hand."

Lily faltered in dusting the grass from her dress and

glared at Mr. Crauford. "Papa is the one who sent me a copy," she said, refusing to give in to the irritation surging through her veins. "The book is hardly scandalous."

"Then he has most certainly failed in his duty to you, and—"

"Sir!"

His jaw slackened at her sharp tone.

"You will not cast any aspersions on Papa. That would not endear you to me." She had been given every advantage possible in education by her father, despite their lack of wealth. He'd encouraged her to read and taught her French and some Greek. Her father had never been a man of great property or fortune, but he had done everything possible to see his daughters looked after. He had never taught her that being able to think for herself was an unladylike thing to do. He supported her dreams wholeheartedly and had never pressured her to find a third husband. Not that he could force her, since she was of age to make her own decisions, but his support meant the world to her.

"You give your opinion too freely, Mrs. Layton," Mr. Crauford said with a pompous air. "I will forgive it in this instance, for you were not reared in a genteel household, but you must learn what proper conduct is for a lady."

His barbed criticism missed its mark, and the man dared to narrow his eyes at her lack of response. She glanced away to find the marquess's arrested stare on her person.

"You're still here," she said and then flushed at her bad manners. "My lord, I—"

He waved away her apology with a suspiciously charming smile. "Pay me no heed, I find I am of a mind to stroll."

She glanced back at the horse grazing the grass.

"Attila is trained to return to the stables when he is riderless. A footman will take him in hand soon," Lord Ambrose said, smiling before tipping his hat and falling back slightly.

The dratted man was endlessly charming and too appealing.

Lily frowned, wondering if it was her imagination or if the marquess had seemed fascinated with the exchange he'd witnessed. Pushing it from her mind, she continued along the path, ignoring Mr. Crauford.

"The weather is very pleasant today," he said after a few minutes.

Lily glanced at the sky, which seemed overcast, and proffered no reply.

"The air is also very pleasant."

She inhaled. "Strange, I only smell manure."

Mr. Crauford looked positively horrified. "*That* is not a topic of discourse for a lady."

A choking sound came from behind her, and she glanced back to see the marquess's eyes dancing with humor. Was he following them? Not that she could protest; it was his land, after all.

Returning her attention to the man walking beside her, she said, "I see. Then what should we talk about?"

He smiled, indulgently, and she sighed at the hollow feeling that rose inside. This was how her last two courtships had unfolded. She had been placed inside a box, where every natural passion and seemingly normal topic of conversations had been suppressed because it was ostensibly unladylike, and she had allowed it. The vicar's constant disparaging words had been wearying. Lily didn't believe all men were that awful, but most did believe that women were to always be proper and that any hint of passion from those gently bred souls indicated a weak and lustful character such as those of loose, immoral leanings possessed.

Mr. Crauford clearly possessed the same sanctimonious attitude. She wasn't certain how to extricate herself from the situation without dissolving into unladylike behavior. *No more.* She was five and twenty, not a wilting flower. "Mr. Crauford...I believe I will continue alone from here."

"No, my dear, there is something I wish to speak of you with," he said with all the importance of a puffed peacock. "I'd thought to take the opportunity while we strolled."

She glanced back, gratified to see the marquess too far back on the beaten path to overhear their conversation. "I truly cannot imagine you have anything to say that I would wish to hear, Mr. Crauford."

His eyes widened. "I do beg your pardon. I believe I misheard."

She shook her head decisively. "I assure you, sir, you did not."

He halted, staring at her as if he had never seen her before. "You have no notion of what I wish to say."

Lily waited with patience she did not feel. Curse this need to always be careful with another's tender feelings. She knew only too well how easy it was to feel injured from a cutting and dismissive tongue. "Forgive me. You are correct."

He nodded, evidently pleased. "I would like to make an offer to your father for your hand in marriage."

She jerked, quite shocked at his pronouncement. "Sir...I...we do not know each other." She had truly thought he would suggest courtship.

"I need a wife, and I've decided you will do. I understand you do not have a dowry, and I am willing to overlook that and your family's lack of connections. I understand there is a second cousin who is a baronet? Lady Ambrose speaks very favorably of you and your family."

"I am thankful for her ladyship's kind sentiments. But I am not interested in remarrying at this time, and even if I were, I would not consent to marry a man who clearly believes it unimportant to get to know the manner of the woman he would take to be his wife. Your cavalier attitude to such a sacred union tells me you do not care about my likes or desires, sir."

For several moments tension crackled in the air. Mr. Crauford drew himself up, ire blasting from his eyes. "Lady Ambrose led me to believe it would be beneficial to marry a woman like you. I can see she was decidedly mistaken. You are too bold with your tongue, which informs me of your clear lack of breeding and of ladylike qualities."

He spun around and froze. Lily glanced back and bit off her cry of dismay. The marquess was right there, and from his cool, watchful gaze, she surmised he had overheard. A mortified flush climbed up her neck.

"A gentleman should never act like a dishonorable buffoon if he is rejected. You bow away with grace," Lord Ambrose clipped icily. "You will apologize to Mrs. Layton."

Mr. Crauford's face went mottled, but he turned to her. "I sincerely apologize, Mrs. Layton."

She nodded, and after a stiff bow in both her and the marquess's direction, Mr. Crauford stormed back toward the manor.

"Thank you," she said, thoroughly shocked he had defended her.

"Think nothing of it. He was unforgivably rude." He looked off into the distance before shifting his piercing regard to her. "If you would allow me to continue as your escort?"

Her eyes widened. "My lord, that is not necessary."

"I do not mind. I was riding to clear my head of thoughts that had been haunting me. Walking with you will do the same, perhaps even more pleasantly."

"I'd planned to venture into the village. If we cut across the field down there," she said, pointing to the track behind the large willow trees, "we would be there in a matter of fifteen minutes."

His head canted left as he considered her.

"It would be my pleasure to escort you, Mrs. Layton," he said.

"Lily," she said, surprising them both. "Please, call me Lily."

"And you must call me Oliver."

"Thank you, my lord."

The charming rogue smiled. "Oliver."

She dipped her head in acquiescence, a grin tugging at her lips. They sauntered toward the village in companionable silence. She was so aware of him her skin felt sensitive, and she was striving hard not to show how nervous she was to be alone with him.

Is it you? Were you inside my body last night, making me wicked with want? The words begged to tumble from her lips, but Lily remained silent. She was silly in her musings; a man of his stature would never make love with a stranger, a woman who for all he knew could be a chambermaid in a secret passageway.

When they came upon a log, he held her elbow and assisted her over, and then resumed, clasping his hands behind him as they continued. Every time she snuck a peek at him, he seemed to be enjoying the peace of their jaunt as much as she was.

They made it to the village without incident but garnered a few curious glances from the villagers. The baker, Mrs. Burke, waved, and Lily returned her greeting. This happened several times before they made it to the small haberdashers at the end of the road. He opened the door for her, and she offered him a quick smile of thanks for his graciousness.

At the threshold, she paused. "I cannot thank you enough for your amiable company, my lord."

"That sounded as if you are about to dismiss me," he drawled, humor dancing in his beautiful eyes.

"I would never be so rude! I simply thought you would like a reprieve. I do have several shops to visit."

"Then lead the way, Lily."

Her heart lurched at the sensual way his voice stroked her name. Lily flushed and hurried into the shop before she said or did something unforgivable.

Chapter Five

Almost two hours after his first encounter with Mrs. Layton—no, *Lily*, Oliver reminded himself—he was still by her side and content to remain there. He had woken up with the need to spend the day with his guests to see if he could unearth any clues to his lover's identity. Breakfast had been a farce, and a peculiar worry had slithered through him. Of the dozen ladies that had been present, none had pulled at him. It was insupportable any present could have been the woman in the secret passageway. Oliver had then decided to take a long ride to clear his head and had been quite pleased to encounter the alluring Mrs. Lily Layton.

She was different from the ladies at breakfast, in a manner that seemed elusive. Her cultured tones spoke of a fine education, her manners were exemplary, ladylike most certainty, but she seemed sturdier. And he did not refer to her mouthwateringly sensual curves. Her grace as she dealt with Mr. Crauford's sanctimonious attitude was admirable and hinted of a backbone. It was entirely strange that Oliver liked her warm company so much.

He'd ignored her puzzled mien as he escorted her from shop to shop, as she bought lengths of calico and laces, some meat pies, knitted stockings for her father, a shawl for her mother, and fruit cake for her nieces. She was too polite to ask why he was accompanying her, perhaps, and she had been scandalized and amused when he took up and carried her basket of assorted goods for her family, who resided nearby. He'd learned her family was made up of her parents and her sister's family, which was comprised of two darling children and an astonishingly wonderful husband, who was the local doctor.

Everywhere she went, someone greeted her and paused to exchange some pleasantries. Some recognized him and hadn't been able to stop staring, and a few had been aghast upon introduction and had scurried away to impart the gossip.

"You are well loved," he murmured, as the current vicar's wife, Mrs. Bainsmith, ended their conversation with several curtsies in his direction before hurrying toward the small bookshop at the corner of the street.

Lily shot him a side-eyed glance. "I was born and raised in this village. The only time I left was right after the vicar died. I resided with one of my cousins in Lambeth for eleven months before I returned."

"You've never explored London?"

"Certainly not to its full potential," she said with a light laugh. "The few times I visited my aunt in Cheapside, I snuck away to visit the shops on High Holborn and Bond Street, where the best dressmakers, tailors, and haberdashers are. I quite scandalized my aunt when I ventured to the fashionable area on my own."

He lifted his chin to the sketchbook clutched in her arms. "For that?"

"Yes."

Several shops past, she had removed her sketchbook to

make space for her items and had been quite reluctant for him to carry it for her. He hadn't insisted, not that he thought she would have caved. Lily seemed like the sort of woman to know herself, considering her refusal of Mr. Crauford's marriage proposal. A strange thing, that. In his experience, a woman of her modest means would have eagerly consented to be the man's wife.

"May I see?"

Vulnerability flashed in her eyes. "My drawings?"

"Only if you are inclined to share."

After a slight hesitation, she held the book out to him. Oliver traded her the basket for it and flipped it open. There were several sketches of dresses, a few he had seen women of high society wearing and others that clearly were not in existence. The lines and style were elegant and creative. "These are very good."

"You know of women's fashion?"

"Enough to know these are exquisite."

A smile lit her entire face, and her unique prettiness stuck him. *Christ.* Her hair gleamed like copper under the sun, and stubborn tendrils had managed to escape her chignon and curl around her cheeks most becomingly. The jolt he felt through his heart was quite unexpected, the twitch in his cock appalling. She had finely arched brows, high cheekbones, and wide and sensual lips.

He wanted to kiss her without consequence.

Wicked images flicked through his mind at the speed of a runaway carriage. Mrs. Layton's lips around his cock, how they would glisten when he kissed and nibbled on them.

Good God, what was wrong with him?

"I believe so, too. The dress your mother wore to last night's supper—I created it," she murmured, pride and satisfaction evident in her tone. "The countess had been reluctant to wear it until she saw my creation."

He recalled the dark green beauty his mother had worn with such grace. "You are incredibly talented."

Lily beamed. "Thank you. I am hoping your mother will be kind enough to recommend me to her set. I am determined to become a sought-after modiste."

He handed her back the drawings and collected the basket once more. "It must have cost you a lot of money to make a dress my mother approved of."

"Almost a year's savings," she replied with a light laugh, walking ahead once more. "But that is the cost of doing business."

"Did my mother compensate you for your creation?"

Her head turned, and startled eyes met his. "It was a gift. I did not expect to be paid."

But his mother should have known what it would have cost a woman of Lily's means to create such a rich garment worthy of a marchioness. Lily was kind and very caring, qualities he deeply admired. It did not escape him that it was her wages she had been using to buy gifts for her family. He admired that she pursued her passion so ardently and wasn't content to accept the life handed to her. It was a pity she wasn't of a different class, for he could see himself wooing a woman like her.

"Ah…here we are," she said with a nervous laugh, waving toward a cottage nestled charmingly off the beaten path. "This is my parents' home, and I…I'm decidedly unsure what is the proper etiquette here. I had no notion the Marquess of Ambrose would spend the day with me in such a menial manner. Not that I imagined you being with me in any other manner," she hurriedly assured him.

A blush pinkened her cheeks, and the most befuddling sensation filled his chest and arrowed down to his cock, hardening it. Shock froze him, and with a will he'd never thought himself capable of, he suppressed the sneaking desire worming through his body for a bloody servant within his household. Wresting his gaze from her beguiling eyes, he scanned the yard. Several chickens clucked, and a young lady was hanging billowing white sheets on a line. As if she sensed his regard, she looked up.

"Lily!" she cried, abandoning her laundry, running over to clasp her in an embrace.

"Mary Rose," Lily scolded. "We've company." She took a steadying breath. "May I present Lord Ambrose. My lord, this is my sister, Mrs. Mary Rose Evans."

"Lord Ambrose!"

His lips twitched as he caught the pinch Lily placed behind her sister's elbow as she gawked. Mary Rose possessed the same dark red hair and brown eyes as Lily and was just as pretty. She quickly curtsied and stammered a greeting. Oliver did his best to put her at ease. He bowed. "I am delighted to make your acquaintance, Mrs. Evans."

"Mamma and Papa have gone to call on Miss Shelby. She's not feeling too well, you see," she said to Lily. Though Mary Rose spoke to her sister, her widened eyes were pinned on him.

What was he doing there with her sister was the clear question. And the answer eluded him, to his great annoyance. "I spy the most charming garden westward," he said abruptly. "I'll leave you to see the arrangements."

"They are my father's pride and joy," replied Lily with a wide smile, and he did his best to not lower his regard to those sweet, pouty lips.

"You'll not find better, my lord."

"If you ladies will excuse me," he said, offering a courteous bow before handing Lily the basket.

They dipped into curtsies, and Oliver walked away, inhaling the mix of fragrances redolent on the air. Life had turned rather strange ever since meeting Mrs. Layton this morning. He had never spent a day so simply but so pleasantly. He hadn't once thought about his estates or burying himself in his darkroom to paint his erotic murals. He hadn't even thought about the young ladies back at Belgrave Manor, all of whom were apparently eminently suited to be his wife. He'd enjoyed Lily's company, and most befuddling, Oliver could not recall having a more amiable time.

• • •

The Marquess of Ambrose had spent the day with her. The very notion still confounded Lily. Even more disturbing, she very much liked his splendid and good-natured company. She had never thought it possible to be at ease with someone so far above her in, well, everything, but not once had he made her feel as if she were inferior.

Her parents had returned home only a few minutes after Lily's arrival. They'd had a pleasant afternoon chat with tea and sandwiches before she had departed. She visited her family weekly, and so enjoyed spending time with them. Their three-bedroom cottage was fully occupied, since it was also her sister and her husband's abode. Her brother-in-law did not make enough of a living to fully support his family. He was terribly kindhearted and did not charge many of his patients who could ill afford medical care. Lily dearly wished to someday earn enough to hire a kitchen maid to help them with the chores.

She had been indecisive about presenting the marquess to her parents, so she'd been relieved to find he had wandered off to the far fields when she finally drummed up the courage to venture outside to offer him refreshment. Lily still couldn't fathom why she had felt so discomfited at the thought of Lord Ambrose in her humble and sparsely furnished home.

Now they were walking at a far brisker pace back to

Belgrave Manor. Thunder rumbled, and she glared at the sky. "I believe it is about to rain." She hurried her steps, almost running. "There is a hunting lodge not too far from here. We could wait out the rain there."

A low curse sounded from the marquess. Lily peered back at him. "What is it?"

There was a dangerous warning in the gaze that stared at her, and she gasped at the dart of heat that quivered to her core. *Dear God. Her desires were ungovernable.* A drop of rain landed on her cheek, and not wasting time to examine the unexpected tension, she ran ahead, uncaring if he followed. Arriving at the hunting cabin, she clambered up the small steps, wrenched open the door, and spilled inside.

"What is this?" The marquess's voice came from behind her.

Lily flushed under his gaze. The hunting lodge was clean, with a fresh bedspread and a curtain by the small window. There was even wood stacked by the fireplace and a few books neatly packed by the small table. She cleared her throat delicately. "The lodge is always empty. I frequently visit here on my off days."

He shot her a considering glance but refrained from commenting.

A burst of raindrops spattered against the glass panes of the window. Several seconds later, it started to storm in earnest. Lily strolled to the lone chair by the window and sat, a trembling breath escaping her when the marquess lowered himself onto the edge of the bed. Why hadn't she ever tried to get another chair for the cabin?

He was a handsome rogue who was a threat to any woman's virtue, even if she were only a paid companion. "Everyone will wonder where we are. I am certain Mr. Crauford relayed to them that we are together."

"It will be evident our delay is because of the inclement

weather."

"Our being alone will be seen as scandalous."

One of his eyebrows arched in apparent incredulity. "I doubt it," he said drily.

Lily flushed. Of course, no one would think it odd a man and his servant had been alone for several minutes. Clearly, it did not even occur to him that people might wonder if they had been improper. "People may still comment," she warned.

"I do not dally with workers in my household."

She gasped and shot him a glare. "I did not ask."

"Ah, I knew what you were thinking. Your eyes are very expressive," he said with a slight frown, as if he were uncomfortable with his assessment.

"And if I weren't part of your household?"

They both froze at her uncensored and improper question. "Forgive me, my lord, I overstepped."

He captured her gaze, and in his eyes, she spied a challenge. "There is nothing to apologize for, Mrs. Layton. I appreciate candor in a woman."

"Even if she is only a servant?"

"Yes."

"Oh."

He considered her for an infinite amount of time, as if she were a perplexing puzzle he was trying to piece together. She dearly wished he wasn't considering answering. It would be too humiliating to listen to his gentle explanations of why he would never have looked at her even if he had encountered her elsewhere. Lily was already aware of the numerous reasons— she was too plump, she had no connections, nor anything particular to recommend her, and she was barren. Dear God, what had possessed her to be so silly with her tongue?

She glared at the slashing rain, which seemed as if it had no intention of relenting soon. She needed to be away from the marquess. She could not dismiss him from any part of her awareness.

"You are a frightfully attractive woman."

She swiveled around at that proclamation. "I... Empty flattery is not needed. I will not wilt away if you are honest."

He chuckled ruefully. "If you knew some of the thoughts I've had of you, Mrs. Layton, I believe you would happily leave my mother's employ."

She stared at him in mute delight. Lily had longed to be admired by a man who saw her in the light of day. If her mysterious lover were to see her now, it didn't correspond that he would still want her. It was a truth she had not dared whisper to herself until now. "Such as?"

"Nothing fit for the ears of a lady such as yourself."

She scowled. "I'm not a prude."

"You are the widow of a vicar."

"And does that mean I am not a woman?"

He dealt her an arrested stare, then Ambrose lifted a brow in challenge. "Are you implying that you have hidden depths?"

A decidedly charged tension permeated the air. She wet her lips. "Most assuredly," she drawled, trying to affect a nonchalant and worldly mien.

He stood with fluid grace and prowled over to her, his eyes stripping her where she sat. Lily fancied he could see the wanton desires in her soul. The marquess peered down at her, a thousand questions in his eyes.

"How deep?"

His tone was more curious than anything else, and she prayed she wasn't blushing.

"I...I slept without a nightgown last night," she said, not wanting to admit to him the far more scandalous thing she had done with her stranger.

Disappointment flashed in his eyes and his shoulders relaxed. "How scandalous."

His mocking drawl had her narrowing her eyes. "I suppose sleeping in the nude is common to a man such as yourself?"

"I daresay it is common among at least half the *ton*, but of course the wife of a vicar would think her naked backside against a silken sheet was appalling."

He scrubbed a hand over his face and moved away, but she heard his muttered curse, which was much filthier than what she had been thinking.

"Forgive me, Mrs. Layton. I was ungentlemanly."

"Truly, I did not mind."

"You're blushing."

"It's the heat," she retorted quickly.

The dratted man laughed, and her body betrayed her by choosing that moment to shiver.

"I've been inconsiderate." He quickly shrugged from his jacket and draped it over her shoulders. A soft moan slipped from her as his wonderful heat enveloped her.

He stilled, and she peered up at him. The manner in which he looked at her was...lustful. Surely it was her imagination. He smiled ruefully, and she felt a familiar quickening low in her belly. Dear heavens, she was truly a harlot. Only last night she had been wrapped in the arms of a stranger, and now there was a wicked temptress inside, urging Lily to step up to the marquess, tip on her toes, and lick along the seam of his lips.

"Why is it important to open a shop?"

Lily stared at him. No one had ever asked her that. The few times she had mentioned her talent to the vicar, she had been berated harshly. Her duties had been to keep their cottage tidy, approve of his sermons, and ensure she was the first in church and the last to depart. Her marriage before that had been sweet and fleeting, and dear Jackson had only wanted to cosset and take care of her, refusing the very notion of her seeking work.

"Sewing is a talent I recognized in myself at the age of twelve. I've spent many days lost in a dream of the fine dresses my sister and I would wear one day," she said with a wistful smile. "That passion simply grew until I had no choice but to follow where it would take me. I purchase fashion sheets when I can. I have a few local patrons who very much love the riding habits and dresses I've created. The magistrate's wife is particularly complimentary. I can make gowns and pelisses to rival London's most famous modistes. I want to see my creations on ladies of high society and featured in the *Lady's Monthly Museum*. A bold aspiration, I know. Is it so silly, do you believe, to want something of your own, to leave your mark on an ever-changing world?"

"No, it's admirable. I will gift you five hundred pounds to open your shop," he said smoothly, his eyes boring into her, his intensity kissing her skin like a warning.

She jerked to her feet as if she were a marionette and him her master. "I beg your pardon, my lord?"

"You heard me."

"That is a fortune."

"It's negligible."

She inhaled sharply, at a loss how five hundred pounds could ever be described as negligible. "I...*why*?"

"I am feeling generous."

Her heart pounded a furious beat. "I cannot accept your generosity. It is inappropriate."

His gorgeous mouth curved into a smile. "Then consider it a payment."

"For what services? Your mother already compensates me quite fairly for my companionship."

He looked thoughtful, then offered a reply. "For helping me select a suitable bride from the dozens under my roof."

"A suitable bride?" she parroted.

"I know my mother has painted your ears with hours of chattering on the type of young lady she would see fill her shoes."

"She has," she said cautiously. The marchioness was very hopeful her son would indeed select a bride and move on to the joyful occasion of producing an heir. "But I do not see how I could possibly be in a position to help." How she dearly wished there was some service she could render. *Five hundred pounds, oh glorious heavens.*

"Finding a suitable bride is no easy task. The sum I offered I gambled away in less than an hour last weekend. It's a piddling amount, Mrs. Layton."

"I think it is incredulous you would need *my* help."

"Perhaps I realize the impossible task in deciding on a bride in one week."

She folded her arms across her chest. "You do have the rest of the London's season. Surely those balls and picnics will have many more wonderful ladies to choose from."

"I am disenchanted with the idea of wading through the marriage mart."

Lily's thoughts raced ahead. "What are the terms?"

His eyebrow arched. "Terms?"

"Will I be paid once you've selected a bride? After you've started courting? An announcement of the engagement?"

He looked faintly shocked at her questions. "No. I am simply paying you for your advice...your opinions on the ladies present in my home."

She nibbled on her lower lip, a nervous habit she'd not shed. "I am not very knowledgeable about ladies of high society, and certainly not your guests. I've spent most of my life here in Hampshire. I've only been to London a few times to visit my aunt and uncle in Cheapside. Being invited to a few of the events of your mother's house party is the most I've mingled with quality."

Nothing she said surprised him, and she frowned, hating the awareness pumping through her. "Was your offer one of charity? Because I assure you, there are far more charitable endeavors worthier of your patronage, and I do not require pity."

"Do not be foolish. Whether or not you have been exposed to the glittering, glamorous world of the *ton* and its season, you have been the wife of a vicar. You, I believe, have an unerring sense of a person's honor and true character."

Dear God, if he knew the truth, she would revolt his noble senses.

"My lord, I—"

"I do not want just a wife...I have certain needs that the young lady must fulfill, and her character must be above reproach."

The dip in his voice when he said "certain needs" intrigued her.

"And what needs are those?" Lily cleared her throat, fighting down the blush at his arrested stare.

"Those I will be able to ascertain for myself. It is your assessment of her character I would find invaluable. Is she kind, intelligent, thoughtful of others? Or is she a shrew... spiteful to those who are not so fortunate? Is she impatient, unfaithful? Are you not able to assess these things about the human heart, as you rightly assessed that Mr. Crauford is not truly interested in your heart and desires? I believe each young lady here will be on their best behavior when I am about."

Of course, he was looking for a virtuous lady.

Who can find a virtuous woman? For her price is far above rubies. The heart of her husband doth safely trust in her so that he shall have no need of spoil. It was a Bible verse her late husband had often quoted to her because he had disapproved severely of the desires of her heart. A lump formed in her throat as she stared at Lord Ambrose helplessly. Of course, he would never deign to even look at a woman like her, one with such an irrepressible need and lustful leanings. What was she even thinking? Even if she had been such a woman, a man like the marquess, so above her in everything, would never regard her in such a manner. "To be clear, my lord, you are simply paying me to be your advisor? Or, to be indelicate, your spy?"

"Yes."

"I see." Except she truly did not. Lily then realized the incredible kindness he was bestowing upon her, for his reasons for gifting her five hundred pounds were rooted in nonsense. He was being charitable and doing his best to show a mien of indifference. The warmth rushing through her heart was surprising. "Thank you," she said, smiling, holding the promise in her heart to help him as best as possible. Lily was unable to believe her good fortune. *Five hundred pounds.* A mere trifle to a man of his stature, but everything to her. She would be able to secure herself a cottage and hire herself a housekeeper and a cook, at least. There would be enough to pay their wages for a year and the rent on the cottage and her shop in town. She could also provide her brother-in-law with a portion to lease the shop he wanted in the village to open a waiting room for his clients to visit him and to stock an apothecary shop to provide medication for the villagers.

"There is something else," Lord Ambrose murmured, staring at her in a way that was decidedly troubling...and arousing.

"Yes?" Then she winced at the breathless quality of her response.

"May I paint you?"

"Paint me?" she parroted inanely.

"Forgive me if I am too forward, but your skin is the most beautiful I've ever beheld, and your smile—I feel it should be immortalized on canvas."

Lily stared at the marquess in ill-concealed shock. "I...I didn't realize you painted," she said, fumbling for equanimity at his praise. Here was a man who didn't think she was too pale, or her lips too full, her mouth too wide. "I've never seen your paintings."

"They are in a private room in the western wing of Belgrave Manor. There are only a few I trust to see them."

"And I am in that category?" she asked skeptically.

"I never said I wanted to show you my work," he replied with a charming quirk of his lips. "Only that I wish for you to sit for me."

"Oh." She winced at hardly containing her disappointment.

"I would make it worth your time, of course," he assured smoothly.

Lily frowned. "In what regard?"

"Another five hundred pounds."

She dropped her basket. He arched a brow and glanced pointedly at it. Before she retrieved it, he stooped and collected her things, picking up her sketchpad, which had spilled out.

"There is no need to be flustered, Mrs. Layton. I promise to leave you in your clothes."

"How remarkably proper," she teased drolly, desperate to disguise her alarm. One thousand pounds was a fortune. "And here I truly believed you had a reputation for being a debaucher of innocents."

"A debaucher most assuredly, but not of the innocent. I wonder, in what category are you? The reserved sort? Or adventurous?"

The desire in his eyes set her world askew. "Are you trying to taunt me into agreeing to your request?"

"Most assuredly. Please also recall my exorbitant offer of

payment."

"And I would only need to sit for a few hours?" Why was her voice hoarse, and why were they standing so close?

"I may require you to be a tad bit scandalous."

Her heart jerked most alarmingly. Lily cleared her throat. "How scandalous?"

"I want your hair loose, fanned across your shoulder... and your feet bare of stockings and boots so I may see your toes and the turn of your ankle. Nothing more."

Nothing more... That was quite scandalous but paled in comparison to how she'd been spending her nights. They stared at each other for an indefinable amount of time. Lily was unsure what was happening, but something had changed between them. It was too vague for her to name, but awareness of it burned along her nerve endings. "Yes, I'll sit for you," she said softly.

A powerful need flared in his gaze before his lids shuttered.

She attempted to reassure herself she did it for the fortune he promised, but deep inside, she knew that to be a lie. It was simply because he asked. How very silly of her to be so thrilled at the notion of being improper with Lord Ambrose.

But inexplicably, he had somehow become a beautiful fire, and she wanted to burn in wanton delight.

Chapter Six

Oliver was not at all indifferent to Mrs. Lily Layton, which was a very startling truth to acknowledge. She knew nothing of the type of woman he wanted to marry, so why had he made his impulsive offer? Because he had wanted to wipe away the bleakness he saw in her eyes, the one that testified she might very well believe she chased an impossible dream. A thousand pounds was a trifling sum to him, but to her, it was freedom, independence, a chance to shine in a life that seemed so dreary for her.

"Is it so silly, do you believe, to want something of your own, to leave your mark on an ever-changing world?"

The stark yearning on her face had struck him hard, momentarily unbalancing him. The rain had slowed to a light drizzle, and they had left the lodge without incident. And he was damned thankful, for never had he wanted to seduce a woman more. Lily walked ahead rapidly, her hips enticing him with their gentle sway. She laughed freely, which delighted him; even the imperfect overbite of one of her teeth, he found charming. If she only knew the lustful dreams she inspired. He clutched his unruly and inappropriate thoughts and buried them in the dark recesses of his mind.

Suddenly, she slipped, and with a soft cry, tumbled onto the muddy earth. He let out a curse and rushed to save her, only to end up in the muck with her. He pushed to his feet and was unable to find purchase on the slippery ground and landed on his ass once more.

A giggle escaped her, and he turned his blackest scowl in her direction. "I fail to see how this situation is amusing, Mrs. Layton."

Her dress had been tossed up to her shin, revealing smooth, pale skin. The lady was without stockings. How scandalous. She had delicate, well-turned ankles, ones he could see crossed behind his neck as he parted the lips of her sex to lick and suck.

Sweet mercy.

"Forgive me. I cannot help noticing how many times I've fallen in front of you today."

Merriment danced in the eyes staring at him, and he could only offer a soft, unintelligent grunt. He was bloody desperate to taste her lips. He'd lost his damn senses to even think of taking advantage of a worker within his household. He assisted her to her feet, finding her adorable when she growled at the sky, which chose to open once more.

"I bid you a good day, my lord!" Then she ran off as if the devil was chasing her, clutching her basket to her chest.

Oliver moved at a leisurely pace, uncaring that the rain was soaking through his clothes. He wanted Mrs. Lily Layton beneath him, rocking on his cock—hard and deep, then soft and sweet, those fine eyes darkening with pleasure.

God's blood. He needed to stay away from her until the aberrant attraction faded. Instead, he would concentrate on finding his mysterious stranger. He only hoped she was as fascinating in the daylight as Lily was.

. . .

Dearest Diary,

*There has always been this wicked desire in me to be
a slave to the pleasures a man can give me. Though,
I very well question if delights between a man and a
woman exist. In all the drawings I've seen, the women
appear as if they are thoroughly enjoying themselves.
Is it selfish of me to want that? Was it terrible of me
to dream last night of Lord Ambrose parting my legs
and kissing my inner thighs? I am terribly attracted
to him, and it seems even my wits have deserted me
when I sleep.*

Oliver gave a rough sigh as he closed the diary, placed it in
the top drawer of his desk, and locked it with a key. Picking
up the whisky he'd been nursing, Oliver finished the drink
in one long swallow. He had spent the better part of the day
in the library poring over investment reports. A luncheon
tray had been sent in by his mother, which he had quickly
consumed without tasting what he ate. Only a couple of hours
after that, he had pushed aside the papers and dismissed his
secretary, admitting his concentration was not at its peak. He
felt like a damned fool, but the dark pull toward the hidden
passageways couldn't be denied.

Yesterday, after his outing with Mrs. Layton, a restless
need had kept him from his bed. The games in the drawing
room, the flirting with the ladies, the conversation at dinner
hadn't left him invigorated, merely bored. Last night, he had
haunted his own house like a specter, roaming those secret
crevices hoping he would encounter his mysterious lady. And
now, instead of directing his effort to his varied business
interests, he was thinking about her.

With a curse, he glanced at the paper on his desk. He was perusing the wrong pages. Oliver moved over to his desk and retrieved the list of viable candidates his mother had made. The young lady at the top of his mother's list was Lady Emma Sinclair, the oldest daughter of the Earl of Preston. The only aspect of their match his mother objected to was that the lady was three and twenty, far too old in her estimation. What nonsense. Oliver liked that she wasn't a fresh debutante and had at least two seasons under her cap. She was very pretty, with a lively and charming demeanor, and he quite enjoyed her intelligence. His mother had given Lady Emma the honor of sitting beside Oliver at last night's dinner, and he had been pleasantly surprised by her charming wit.

He liked her, yet he was not attracted to her gentle beauty.

His mysterious lover was one of the widows under his roof. But only one had made it on to his mother's list: Lady Falconbridge. She was young, four and twenty, well-connected in the *ton*, and had the bluest of blood, as the daughter of a duke.

Without warning, the library door opened, and his sister sailed inside.

Oliver placed the list on the desk and sat on the surface. "Have your manners departed you, Lucinda?"

"I knew you were in here alone," she said with an impish smile, dark blue eyes so much like his own dancing merrily. "Oliver, please, will you speak with Mother? Within a few months, I'll be seventeen, and I dare say I am responsible enough to attend a ball held in our own home."

"You haven't had your come out yet."

Her eyes flashed, and her chin tilted stubbornly. "When did you get so priggish?"

"Lucinda," he started warningly.

She hurried over to him. "Oh dear, it was the word priggish, wasn't it? Mrs. Layton has a delightful way with phrases, and I find myself borrowing a few."

Mrs. Layton. Not the woman he wanted to think about now. He'd already endured a frustrating night, vacillating between wanting her and craving his mysterious lover. There had even been a time he wondered if she could *be* her. He'd dismissed the ridiculous notion, of course. He had been in her presence for hours yesterday. Surely, he would have detected something familiar? The rasp of her voice, that elusive scent of honeysuckle.

"There will be no one for you to converse with."

She wagged a finger. "That is not true. Lady Henrietta and I are very close in age. She is only one year older."

Swift distaste filled him that a young lady so close to his sister's age was on his mother's list. Christ. Such innocents shouldn't be marred by the kind of cravings he harbored in his soul. He mentally struck another woman from his list.

"I will speak with Mother."

"Oh, Oliver, thank you."

He grunted as she flung herself at him and hugged him with exuberance. She released him and pressed a kiss to his cheek.

"There is more."

He arched a brow.

"Charlotte is here."

"When did she arrive?"

Lucinda frowned "Only an hour past. She is with mother. I…think she is unhappy, and Mother seemed angry. I heard her tell Charlotte that she has a duty to her husband, and she should return to Chadwick Hall and await her Lord Beresford."

A cold knot formed in Oliver's gut. His sister Charlotte was two and twenty and had been married to Viscount Beresford for three years. She had declared herself in love with him, and the viscount had seemed equally besotted.

Oliver had given his blessings to their union despite his mother's disgruntlement, as she had wanted her daughter to marry the Duke of Milton.

"I'll speak with Charlotte," he promised. "Now go, and stop eavesdropping."

Lucinda giggled and all but skipped from the room.

A full minute did not pass before a gentle knock sounded on the door. Charlotte. His two sisters could not be more different. Whereas Lucinda was irrepressible, Charlotte was very sweet and well comported. Oliver could not recall ever hearing a cross word from her, nor would she ever think to just barge in on him in his private sanctum.

"Come in, Charlotte."

The door opened, and she strolled in, her face lit with a smile. Both he and Charlotte favored their father, inheriting his dark hair and cobalt-colored eyes.

"I see Lucinda informed you I am here."

Was that strain in her voice?

"She did."

Charlotte closed the door and faltered. "I sat for a while with Mother in the drawing room. I fear she is not very pleased to see me."

"Nonsense. You are always welcome at Belgrave Manor."

She visibly swallowed and rested a hand on her gently rounded stomach. Her eyes were wounded, and his heart froze.

"Is the baby unwell?"

"No such calamity, I assure you, dear brother," she said with a smile that wobbled.

In her eyes, he spied shame and pain. He held open his arms and she rushed into them.

"There now," he said. "Just tell me what's the matter this time, and I'll sort it out."

"It's John," she murmured on a sob. "I...I've heard

rumors that he has a mistress."

That bloody blackguard. Oliver had warned him when he handed his sister over into his care how precious she was to be treated.

"Rumors are vile things, and you know, oftentimes, they are incorrect."

She burrowed even closer against his chest, silent tears jerking her shoulders.

"I confronted him, and he refused to have any such discussion with me. He was angry, and he left for Town. I packed my trunks and came here. Oh, Oliver, I cannot go back, my heart and my pride have been broken."

He kissed her hair. "I'll go and see him."

She pulled from his arms. "Will you?"

"Yes. I'll leave first thing in the morning for London. And I'll not return without him. And I promise you, if somehow there is a mistress…"

She flinched as he rubbed soothing strokes on her shoulder.

"If there is another woman, and I doubt it highly, for John dotes on you, I promise he will put an end to it."

By any means necessary.

His throat tightened at the trust with which she peered up at him. With a soft sigh, she clutched him in another fierce hug.

"I can imagine what Mother has told you about duty and whatnot. But you'll stay here for as long as need be."

"Thank you, Ol. I love you."

"I love you, too," he murmured. "I'm sure you are weary from your journey. You should wash up."

There was a now a happy light in her eyes that he was well pleased to see. A few seconds later, he was once again alone, restless energy coursing through his veins. If the viscount truly had a lover, his gentle and trusting sister would be shattered for a long time yet. And he would have to be harsh with a friend, perhaps even breaking a bone or two to get his message across.

Oliver scrubbed a hand over his face, ruthlessly suppressing the violent thoughts.

Ignoring the need to enter the hidden passages once more, he exited the library and made his way down the hallway to the winding staircase that led to the west wing. Several minutes later, he reached a room only he had the keys to. Dipping into his pocket, he withdrew the key and opened the door, then stepped into his dark room. He sauntered to the drapes and tugged them open, washing the room with sunlight. Several paintings graced the walls, all unbearably erotic drawings that he had done.

He strolled over to his latest work, frowning at an anomaly he spied. The lady draped over a chaise lounge with her ass arched delightfully in the air had red hair, brown eyes…and sweet lips. Oliver sighed. How had he not realized he'd imbued Mrs. Layton in his paintings? He searched the other canvases, his shoulders eventually relaxing. In all the other paintings the women depicted so lasciviously had their faces slightly blurred. Only that one had the faint impression of his mother's lady's companion.

He walked over until he stood directly in front of it. He had captured a mischievous smile he had never seen from her. Lust coiled in his gut, dark and inviting, as he accepted the truth of his desires. He wanted to ruin her sensibilities. He imagined her lips sliding over his cock; it was her pussy he wished to ride for hours…and then seduce her into oiling her forbidden rear entrance and sliding his cock deep.

God's blood.

As soon as the house party was over, he needed to make his way to Town and away from Belgrave Manor. Otherwise, he would certainly succumb to his dark needs, ruining a good woman who did not deserve to be used and discarded after he had slaked his lust.

• • •

Oliver departed Belgrave Manor at dawn and arrived in Town a few hours later. Walking up to his sister and her husband's townhouse in Mayfair, he hammered on the knocker. The door opened, and the butler stepped back.

"Lord Ambrose, may I take your coat and hat?"

Oliver handed them over. "Is the viscount in?"

The butler bobbed. "Yes, your lordship. He is in the breakfast room."

"No need to announce me," he said, making his way down the hall. The last time Oliver visited had only been a few weeks ago, when his sister had invited her family to Town for a small dinner party and then gave them the welcome news of the expected addition to their family.

Reaching the breakfast room, he spied John with a pressed newspaper close to his face. He lowered it and glanced up.

"Ambrose!" Apprehension flashed in his eyes. "Is it Charlotte?" he asked, a worried frown appearing.

Oliver lowered himself into the chair closest to the viscount and pinned him with a hard stare. John was only two years older than Charlotte and had always been a steady and good-natured sort. Oliver thought it unlikely he had a mistress, but then, many men and lords, if not all, truly believed keeping a *chère amie* was as necessary as breathing air. The bloody idiots.

That his father had not respected and cherished the vows made to his wife was one of the things that had most disappointed Oliver. The man had lectured often on matters of honor, yet had been so blind to his own lack of honor to his vows that he became the least likely candidate Oliver would listen to. He had tried to understand it from his father's perspective, but as he'd grown older, he'd come to see how ungentlemanly and disgusting it was to make promises to a person and so casually break an oath for fleeting pleasures of the flesh.

"Your viscountess arrived at Belgrave Manor with packed trunks."

The man blanched. "She's left me? Why would she do that?"

"Because she believes you have betrayed her trust and love." The hurt in his sister's eyes had been painful to witness.

John froze, and Oliver's gut tightened at the flash of guilt in the man's eyes.

"I've done nothing of the sort," he said stiffly.

"Do you remember the conversation we had in my study when you asked my permission to court her?"

The viscount looked away, took a steady breath, and then met Oliver's gaze.

"I do. You promised broken bits if I ever hurt Charlotte."

"Do you have a mistress?" Oliver clipped icily.

The man had the grace to flush. "I...I've approached Mrs. Dorothy Williams, but we haven't finalized an agreement."

Oliver bit back a curse. "Why would you do this to Charlotte?" Even though he suspected. That fear of tainting a genteel wife with his baser urges had him haunting his own damn home for a stranger. But if the viscount struggled with a similar belief, the man had better learn to govern his lustful cravings. Oliver would not idly stand by and see his sister endure the same pain and shame that had followed their mother for years.

The viscount couldn't meet his eyes for a few moments. "It's because I love her."

The damn fool. "I don't believe I've heard greater

nonsense."

Beresford tugged at his cravat. "I couldn't bring myself to subject her to...to...God's blood, man, you *know*! I love Charlotte more than anything in my life, and I would not hurt her for the world. She is with child and must be treated with all gentleness and respect."

There was no doubt the blathering fool thought that because she was in the family way, they could not be intimate. "Yet you have done so with your thoughtless and selfish action. I gather it would not trouble you if she decided to take a lover?"

The viscount half lurched from his chair, his hands fisted on the table. "I would kill any man," he breathed, his voice raw, panic flashing in his eyes.

"Yet you expect her to accept your infidelity with genteel grace." Very much like how Oliver's mother had lifted her chin at her husband's numerous indiscretions. "I could hear my sister's sobs last night as she cried into her pillow. I'm mildly surprised I've not put a bullet in you," he murmured, low and hard.

Beresford paled. "She cried?"

"For hours."

The fool dropped his forehead into his hands. "I've...I've not slept with Mrs. Williams. I visited her last evening, but I spent the time talking about Charlotte. Dear God, I've been a fool."

"That you have."

"I'll head down with you to Hampshire."

Oliver stood, and the viscount lurched to his feet. Oliver grabbed the lapels of his jacket in a tight, merciless grip and dragged him close. "If my sister is not of a mind to forgive you, you'll be leaving without her. And I'll not compromise my stance. It is because she loves you that I haven't ripped your cock from your body."

His eyes widened in ill-concealed alarm. "I'm obliged to you, Ambrose."

With a soft grunt, he released him. "My sister has more strength than you credit her for. She is sweet and gentle, but she is also fierce and courageous. She is not a wilting ninny. Reserve all your passions for her. Speak with her about your fears, and she may very well surprise you."

And perhaps any woman Oliver should take to be his wife he could do the same, communicate about everything. His heart hammered at the notion. Maybe he was the damn fool searching for his midnight lover. What if he found her and she lacked the connections and reputation to be his marchioness? Worse, what if she lacked the character that would recommend her to be his partner. He hungered for more than just a lusty woman to wet his cock whenever or however he wanted. An eventual friendship in his marriage was quite important to him.

"Ensure that you tell your viscountess all you wish to explore with her. And then you will be mindful of her sensibilities, but do not hesitate to invite her with you on any adventures. And if Charlotte should not want to explore with you, by God, you will respect her decision and cherish the promises you made to her."

Beresford nodded stiffly, and Oliver walked around him. "I'll see myself out."

He collected his hat and coat, departed the townhouse, and strolled toward his waiting carriage. He vaulted inside and ordered the carriage to St. James Square. He would stay the night in town, perhaps even visit White's or Lady Pennant's masquerade ball, which promised to be an event of delightful debauchery.

It was at Lady Pennant's masquerade last year he and Radbourne had been snared in Lady Wimbledon's erotic wiles. Oliver frowned. No anticipation rushed through him.

He felt no temptation to participate.

Large brown eyes framed by long delicate lashes floated through his thoughts. Mrs. Lily Layton. And at once, he decided to head back to Belgrave Manor first thing in the morning. He was faintly shocked it was not thoughts of finding his mysterious lover that drew him.

How I want you...

Clenching his teeth until they ached, he vowed then to resist, lest he destroy his honor, her reputation, and her modest sensibilities. He would head back to his townhouse now and retire to his bed, where he suspected he would dream of the wicked debauching of his brown-eyed tormentor, and Oliver would do his damnedest to ensure they remained only that—lustful fantasies of ravishing Lily Layton—and nothing more.

Chapter Seven

The night of the auspicious ball arrived without much fanfare. Elegantly garbed couples waltzed under the light of dozens of candles in the crystal chandeliers overhead. Lily strolled the fringes of the crowded dance floor, keenly observing the variety of styles the ladies wore. The ballgowns were glorious, and she felt pleased with the alterations she had done to the dress the marchioness had given her. Lily knew she looked fetching, as evidenced by a few admiring glances aimed in her direction. Mr. Crauford made a concentrated effort to not look her way, and the marchioness had raised a brow at the obvious tension between them.

Over an hour had passed since the dancing started, and no one approached her. Lily wasn't sure if she felt relieved or disappointed. She had to remind herself of her purpose in attending.

A ripple went through the small group of women reposing on chairs a few feet from her.

"How magnificent Lord Ambrose appears tonight."

"The rumor he is hunting for a wife has set London on its

ears. Lady Shelton sent me clippings of several newspapers that say a close source has revealed Ambrose desires for a wife and children," a voice tittered. "Maryann is well suited to be a marchioness, and I believe my daughter, more than any other young lady here, stands a chance."

A shiver of some unfathomable sensation moved through Lily, and she scanned the small gathering until she found him. Not that it had been hard; he seemed to be the only gentleman standing with at least four ladies, all beautiful and elegantly poised, around him. The marquess was impeccably dressed in dark trousers and jacket, a silver waistcoat, his cravat immaculately tied. The delight she felt at seeing him was disconcerting. She had missed his presence this past couple of days and had scolded herself quite fiercely for the desires welling inside her for this man. She could entertain no misconception of his interest in walking with her. That way would surely lead to disaster.

"I have it on the highest authority that the marquess commands at least three hundred thousand pounds a year, and that does not include his business investments, just the estates. He is indecently rich."

Lily's eyes widened. That was a fortune she could not comprehend. No wonder he thought so little of "paying" her one thousand pounds. She hadn't seen him since, for he had vanished to Town. Bereft at the emptiness she'd felt, and eager to purge Lord Ambrose from her thoughts, she had made her way down to the stairs and hovered near the library several times. The desire to visit those hallways, and perhaps encounter her clandestine lover again, had been a lesson in denying temptation.

"He cuts quite a dashing and commanding figure, doesn't he?" that same person said, her voice rich with admiration. "And it is quite evident he is truly ready to settle down. I'd thought it a rumor."

Lily recognized Lady Falconbridge, the wealthy widow of a viscount who had died in a carriage accident three years past. The way she ogled Lord Ambrose signaled she would be a contender for his affections. She had also been on Lady Ambrose's list for suitable ladies for her son, simply because she had given the viscount an heir and a spare before his death. Lady Falconbridge's greatest value as a wife for a nobleman had been proven with the fruits of her womb.

Lily's eyes smarted, and she strolled away, not caring to hear any more about the marquess. She did turn her attention to him, admiring his powerful and graceful form, as he swept one of the most ravishing ladies she had ever seen across the ballroom. How wonderful they looked together.

With great reluctance, she tore her regard from the dancing couple. She mustn't be so obvious in her admiration, considering she lingered on the marquess. A footman passed, and she snatched a glass of champagne and sipped the golden liquid. After observing another three sets of dancing, it was distressing to admit she was frightfully bored. There was simply nothing for her to do. Others around her laughed and chattered away with great animation, but no one engaged with her. She didn't belong, and everyone knew.

For politeness's sake, she would wait a few more minutes, then slip away to the library and perhaps select a book to read until sleep beckoned. Or venture once more into the darkened passage…

Remembered pleasure stroked her skin, and there was a pleasant tightening in her womb. Good lord, could she risk it again? What if she encountered the unknown lover once more? Lily closed her eyes, reluctantly admitting that was what she wanted. To feel his thick cock part her core once again, satisfying her with that pained bliss that had made her shatter with such intensity.

Could she truly do it again?

And what if he isn't there?

But the more terrifying question was, what if she encountered him once more?

If he's there, I'll take him as he'll surely take me.

A few hours from now, she would once again walk that fine edge between freedom and ruin…

It was going to be a long night.

. . .

Oliver twirled around the ballroom with Lady Penelope for the second time. They had been paired in a quadrille and now a waltz. His mother had waylaid him earlier, imploring him to first dance with Lady Penelope. He hadn't told his mother he had already struck her from the list. Though he had sought out her help, he would not give her a daily update on his pursuits. He had partnered with Lady Emma earlier in a game of croquet, had complimented the watercolors she'd painted, and his mother had been too obvious in her delight. He had overheard a few other ladies speculating whether he had made his choice.

The plan had been to dance and mingle with the widows present, but Oliver found it hard to concentrate on the matter at hand. Since he'd spied Lily, his mind had blanked. What was she doing at the ball looking so bloody appealing? She wore a rose-colored gown that hugged her figure most enticingly. Her mane of dark red hair was piled high atop her head in intricate curls, with several wisps artfully arranged to drape across her forehead and down to her shoulder. With no accessories except for a pair of white gloves, she was possibly the only woman at the ball so unadorned. No pearls, diamonds, or rubies circled her throat, and he wished he could lay them at her feet. A ridiculous desire.

She stood on the sidelines, looking so lovely…and perhaps

a bit lonely. He frowned, noting the half smile on her lips and the yearning way she stared at the dancing couples—though, he thought it likely she could be admiring their apparel. She collected another glass of champagne and then moved to a chaise and sat.

"Would you like to take a turn in the garden after our waltz, my lord?" Lady Penelope asked, dragging his attention back to her. Oliver hoped he hadn't been obvious in his admiration of Lily. He peered down at the beautiful lady in his arms, noting the haunting sadness in Lady Penelope's eyes.

"Are you still in love with Lord Bainbridge?"

Her lips parted in a silent gasp, and her eyes widened. "My lord! I..." She struggled for equanimity as her eyes welled with tears. "It does not signify. My parents won't approve the match."

"He is working like a madman to bring his estates back from the brink of ruin. He does not say it, but I know his relentlessness is because he fears you will wed another before he succeeds."

Hope flared in her eyes. "Truly?"

"Yes."

Her lips trembled with a smile. "I do not care if he is not wealthy."

"Then fight for him, wait for him, do not give in to your parents' demands, for we only live once. It would be foolish, I believe, to marry elsewhere when your heart is irrevocably in love with another."

She visibly swallowed. "And you do not think he hates me for rejecting him before?"

"No."

"Thank you, my lord. I will not forget your kindness," she said huskily, peering over his shoulder to Bainbridge, who lounged in a darkened corner watching her with astonishing intensity.

"Discreetly go to him, give him hope."

A wide smile of joy appeared on her lips, rendering the lady exquisite. "I will, thank you."

Their dance ended, and he escorted her to the sidelines. His mother lifted her chin toward Lady Emma and Miss Julianna Darby, but Oliver paid her no heed. Instead, he made his way over to Lily.

She shot to her feet as he stood in front of her. Her eyes were alert, curious even. "My lord," she said, dipping in an elegant curtsy.

"Mrs. Layton."

Her gaze flicked around the room and then back to him. "Upon my word, I believe the entire room is staring at you," she whispered, her cheeks flushing a becoming pink. "Why are they doing that?"

"They are curious as to why I've approached you. They are also staring at you."

"They are impolite, that's what they are."

"You are commanding attention because you are so beautiful."

She gave him a bright, glorious smile. "Thank you, my lord." Then she frowned. "Why have you approached me? Your mother is watching us, and I can see your sister peeking from behind the potted plant on the terrace."

There was an allure to their directness. "May I have the honor of the next dance? I believe another waltz will be announced."

She went motionless, her mouth frozen in a small *O*. "I don't know what to say," she finally said, sounding perplexed and perhaps thrilled. "This is so unexpected, your lordship."

"You could say yes."

A beautiful smile curved her lips, drawing his eyes to the small overbite of her teeth. She was so different from the ladies of society in the room. Oliver knew if any had that small imperfection, they would forever smile with their lips sealed. Excitement brought out the beauty in her eyes, the flush on her cheeks.

She cleared her throat. "I would be delighted, my lord. It was only yesterday I practiced with Lady Lucinda, so you will forgive me if I accidentally step on your toes."

Suddenly, he felt like a heel. It had never occurred to him she might not know how to dance. "I'll catch you if you stumble."

She stared up at him, her golden-brown eyes raging with emotion, and a question glowed in the depth of her gaze, one he was unable to answer. It was simply important to him she understood he would be there if she faltered.

He held out his hand, and she came willingly to him. Oliver was almost amused at the shock he could feel rippling through the ballroom. Even those who were also taking to the dance floor sent curious glances their way. Perhaps it would even be mentioned in the gossip columns that Lord Ambrose had danced with his mother's companion at his ball.

He settled his hand against her waist, and she placed her gloved hand on his shoulder. She felt perfect in his arms. *Too perfect.* The strains of the violins leaped to life, and Lily flowed beautifully in his arms. She attempted to lead him, and it became clear she had been the dominant partner when she practiced with his sister. He tugged Lily closer, subtly shifting the dynamics so she understood who was in charge of their sensual and elegant waltz across the ballroom floor.

A smile curved over her lips before it bloomed into a wide grin. "This is glorious, Oliver."

The devil in him urged him to pull her in even closer, and he gave in to the temptation, even knowing the eyes of the ballroom were upon them. Sweet and alluring, her subtle fragrance of lavender stirred him. Her gaze never left him, and for an impossible moment, Oliver felt as if they were in the room alone as he drowned in the beauty of her eyes. Had he ever seen a lady this intelligent and curious, or with such a bewildering mix of innocent and inviting carnality?

It wasn't his fevered imagination that something wicked lurked in her eyes. Oliver gritted his teeth until his jaw ached. This blasted attraction was unfounded, and he needed to take control of his desires.

While he had admired his father and emulated his dedication to their estates and his acumen in business, there the similarities would end. Oliver would not dally with a worker in his household, who would surely feel pressured to accept any sexual advances he would make. Something his father had never cared to consider as he seduced maid after maid, taking cruel advantage of their situation and humiliating his marchioness. It pained Oliver to acknowledge that some of his father's unruly desires had taken hold of him, for he dearly wanted to ravish Mrs. Lily Layton with his tongue, fingers, and cock until she was limp from pleasure.

In a desperate bid to center his thoughts on anything but how delectable she appeared, he said, "Have I ever thanked you for all that you do for my mother, Lily?"

A blushed worked its way up her neck. "Your gratitude is not necessary. I am paid."

"I would like to think it is more than that. My mother genuinely likes you, and I can see you hold similar affections."

She arched a delicate brow. "Yes, she likes me so much she is firing me."

He faltered briefly, but caught himself, expertly twirling her past several couples. "I wasn't aware my mother was letting you go."

"She believes I should marry, and that I am wasting away as her companion. My replacement will be here at the end of the month."

His stomach clenched into hard knots at the idea of her marrying, but he brushed it aside. "Ah, to Mr. Crauford. You haven't told her that you've rejected his advances, and he is too proud to mention that he has failed. You have a difficult task ahead of you, persuading my mother you have no wish to wed him or any other man. Her matchmaking fervor is terrible to behold."

Lily scowled. "I have no wish to marry again, and I daresay the marchioness will have to respect my position."

"You are still young. I'm sure the vicar wouldn't have wanted your unhappiness."

"It would be silly of me to even think of the wishes of a dead man," she said with a definite twinkle in her eyes. "I...I simply do not think it is for me. I have been married twice."

Twice? "How old are you?"

She pursed her lips. "Five and twenty."

"Good God, and you've been widowed twice?"

Shadows lingered in her eyes. "I have."

"May I ask about your first marriage?"

Surprise flashed in her eyes. Dark red tendrils floated around her delicate face as she peered up at him. "We grew up in the village together. Our mothers were the best of friends. I truly liked him and enjoyed his company. It seemed natural we would marry after we came of age. I married Charlie when I was seventeen. Several months later, he bought a junior commission for the war." She cleared her throat. "He never came home. His family mourned his sacrifice and celebrated his courage. I, too, grieved him, for he had been a kind and gentle soul who deserved much more from life. A few years later, I married the local vicar."

A small smile on her lips as she spoke of her first husband implied fond memories. Yet a shadow flashed at the mention of the vicar. "How long were you married to the vicar?"

A slight frown marred her lovely brows. "Three years."

"So, you remarried at twenty."

Her lips twitched. "That I did, my lord."

"I'm sorry for your losses. You have endured much for one still so remarkably young," he said softly.

"Thank you."

And now his mother and possibly her society urged her to find a third husband. Yet the strong beauty before him did not appear as if she needed another spouse.

He spun her in a graceful arc, and the only indication of any nervousness was the tightening of her fingers on his shoulder.

She cleared her throat delicately. "I believe we must discuss the preposterous notion of me helping you find a wife amongst your guests."

"And to think I thought it a most ingenious suggestion."

"I know you only made such an offer so I would take the money. I am grateful for your kindness, truly, but I do not mix well with your society, and the small observations I've made tonight cannot help in your pursuits."

He needed a moment to collect himself. She had seen through his offer, and he was damn glad she hadn't taken offense to his charity. He suspected she never asked anyone for anything and much preferred to earn her way in the world. Quite admirable and so very different from many people he knew. It was irrational to feel disappointment at the thought she would not take his money to further her dreams. "Your honesty is charming, Mrs. Layton. Many would pretend to dole advice to collect on the bounty offered."

She lifted her chin quite arrogantly, further baring the swanlike grace of her neck. "I am not like many others."

"I am beginning to see that," he murmured. "You could still help."

She rolled her eyes. "I doubt it. The many ladies here tonight have not deigned to converse with me. And I cannot imagine how I would get close enough to anyone to determine their character."

"I could help you narrow the list."

Her eyes widened. "How?"

"I think we could start with the widows—"

Her gasp cut him off. "You are seeking a widow for your next wife?"

He went silent for a brief moment, assessing her wide-eyed expression. "As a man of the world, I think it wise to marry a lady with experience."

The pulse fluttered wildly at her throat. "I did observe you conversing with two widows earlier. Were they to your liking?"

No. He hadn't felt any spark or even a physical attraction. The conversation had been mundane, their dulcet tones entirely unfamiliar. Their scent unrousing. "They were not," he admitted softly.

She made no reply, and they silently twirled to the graceful waltz.

"You are truly an apt pupil, Mrs. Layton. You dance beautifully."

Another radiant smile bloomed on her lips. "Flattery will get you everything, my lord."

"Then will you sit twice for me and accept my payment of one thousand pounds for the privilege?"

"Two different paintings?" she whispered as if scandalized. There was a becoming flush on her cheeks, and a nameless hunger tore through his heart.

"Yes."

Her eyes searched his with an intensity he did not understand. How he wished he could read her thoughts.

"If you inform me where I should meet you, my lord, and what time, I shall be there."

Fierce anticipation rushed through him. "Thank you."

"I am very curious to see your paintings, if you will permit me the honor."

How shocked her sensibilities would be if she saw his gallery. "I mostly paint classical nudes."

She visibly swallowed. "I see. And has…anyone ever posed for you in the nude?"

There was that dark, inviting desire coiling in his gut again. "A few."

Something elusive pooled in her gaze, and she considered him in silence for a few moments. "And if I should ask you to paint me like that, would you take affront, or be intrigued?"

It was his turn to stumble ever so slightly. Who was this woman he held in his arms? The few women he had painted, they had frolicked in debauchery together, but there was nothing sinful or depraved about the widow of a bloody vicar. Unless…

He held her gaze for an infinite time until her lids lowered. The gentle upward curve of her lips hinted at wicked amusement, and devil take it, Oliver was captivated.

Their dance ended all too soon, and regret sliced through him that he wouldn't be spending more time with her tonight. Brushing aside the perplexing desire, he escorted her to the sidelines. She dipped in a graceful curtsy, and with a nod, he departed. It was tempting to claim her for another dance, but that would only stir unnecessary rumor. And he was on another mission tonight.

Which one of the widows present was his mysterious lover?

Oliver spent the next two hours mingling, dancing, and chatting, disliking that he wanted to be elsewhere. He bantered with several women and found it quite unlikely that any of them were the woman in the secret passage.

Bloody hell. Who are you? Where are you?

Chapter Eight

Muted strains of laughter, accompanied by the orchestra, drifted through the oak door of the library, despite it being four in the morning. His mother's guests were determined to party until dawn. Oliver had left the ball a couple of hours ago and had tried to immerse himself first in a book and then some business ledgers, to no avail. Restless energy had pounded through him, and he'd escaped to the lawns outside, inhaling the crisp night air into his lungs, trying to center his thoughts. It hadn't worked. He'd returned inside, determined to pen a few letters, and when he'd entered the library, Mrs. Layton had been curled in the sofa closest to the roaring fire, sleeping, a book lying on her chest.

Oliver had snuck away and bounded up the stairs for his canvas and easel, a few oils and brushes. He couldn't explain the hunger that had seized him. He had sat on the edge of his desk, the canvas mounted on the easel, and with raw but sensually soft strokes, he'd started to paint her.

She'd come awake as if she sensed his intensity. Her movements had been slow, carnal, like a feline as she'd uncurled and sat up. Oliver had paused, poured whisky into two glasses, and handed her one without speaking.

The woman tentatively sipping whisky before him, to Oliver's thinking, was the embodiment of temptation. The elegant arch of her throat moved as Lily swallowed the last of the drink, and she leaned to the side and rested the glass on a small table.

Silence lingered. He made no effort to speak, and he was pleased she did not shatter the intimacy. A stroke of the brush that he could imagine to be his fingers on her soft skin glided over the canvas. She sat, quite prim and proper on the edge of the sofa, her hands clenched on the cushions, her body taut, a tightly coiled spring waiting for release. Her eyes were wide and luminous as they stared at him, her lush, rosy lips were wet and glistening, for she had licked them several times in apparent nervousness.

"Are you nervous being alone with me?"

She shook her head, and he wished her movements would loosen the intricate hairstyle and let it tumble across her shoulders. Somehow, he knew the waves would be glorious.

"I need the words, Lily." Inexplicably, he needed to know she felt safe in his presence.

Another glide of her tongue along her lower lip. "I am not afraid or anxious." Her answer was husky and filled with an emotion he could not decipher.

Something elusive whispered through him, but it was warm and heady. It had been a long time since he felt this way with a lady companion. There was no boredom, only a sense of muted arousal, anticipation, a peculiar sense of something new hovering on the periphery of his awareness of the woman before him.

"Relax your shoulders."

She unclenched the cushions and, with a whispering sigh, leaned back on the sofa.

He wanted to deck her in an emerald necklace and paint her naked. Immediately he rejected the thought. She should be painted with a hint of mystery, a sensual smile on those lips, invitation and innocence glowing from her golden eyes, her neckline only slightly lowered, but her puckered nipples evident.

"Is this to your satisfaction?" she asked, looking self-conscious.

"Almost. Remove your slippers. Cross your legs at the knee...and allow your gown to drag up and bare your ankles to my eyes."

Her breathing fractured and a pretty flush of pink bloomed across her cheeks. What would she taste like? A mere brush of his lips on hers would solve that mystery. Would she slap his face or welcome his touch? Something in her eyes invited him over, and he wondered if that was simply a fanciful hunger. Oliver waged a fierce battle with temptation and the needs beating at him. Perhaps painting Lily Layton would be the gravest of mistakes. He cursed under his breath. "Perhaps it was not wise for me to start painting you tonight. You must be tired."

She stared at him for a long moment, her lips slightly parted, before flashing him a small smile. Then she stood. "Sleep well, my lord."

He watched her leave, unable to wrest his gaze away from her. The door closed with a soft click, and Oliver released the breath he hadn't realized he held. Putting away his oils and brushes, he strolled to the sideboard and poured another drink, then another, pushing all thoughts of Lily Layton from his thoughts.

Unable to halt the need, he made his way to his desk and plucked the diary from the top drawer. Taking a steady breath, he flipped the diary open and picked a random entry.

Dearest Diary,

How I wish to indulge in the simple pleasure of standing in the rain or perhaps reposing on the wet grass, my face lifted to the heavens, the feel of soft wind on my face, the beat of the rain as it pounds against my skin. I long for freedom, to do as I wish without any rebuke. I've no husband now, so why do I hesitate? Should I wish to eat dessert before the main course, I shall do so. If I wish to run in the rain or swim in the lake, then I will. And if I desire to touch myself while I think of Ambrose…then I shall, without any guilt. Why does he entice me so? Why does he haunt my dreams when I know full well a man such as the marquess would never consider a woman of my circumstance for his lover?

Giving a rough sound, he closed the diary and put it back in the drawer. What was her circumstance? Nothing in her words ever revealed an inkling of her identity or her connections. With impatient movements he shed his jacket, waistcoat, cravat, and his boots, leaving them on the library floor. He opened a small, carved wooden box by the inkwell, removed a cheroot, and lit it. Oliver stared at the bookcase for several minutes and was still unable to convince himself to retire to his bedchamber. Tonight would be the third night Oliver would haunt his house, hoping—more like praying—that he would encounter his secret lady.

Oliver ground the root of the cheroot in an ashtray, then swallowed the rest of his whisky before placing the glass on the desk.

He pushed off the desk and prowled over to the secret panel. Before he could stop himself, he opened it and stepped into the dark passageway. He took no candlestick, at home with the darkness, and with sure feet, he made his way along the silent corridor. He traversed the length, and it was not long before he realized he was alone. There was no one lingering in these passages. With a groan of defeat, he leaned against the wall and tipped his head back, staring into the abyss. Why was he making it an obsession to find her?

Suddenly, an awareness rippled through him, and he froze, hardly daring to hope. He sensed her approach, and triumph sang through him.

"You're here." Her voice was husky, bold and daring, and he instinctively knew this was unlike her.

"Yes. I've returned a few nights since."

A swift inhalation. "I made no promises."

"Why are you here?"

"I couldn't sleep," she said. "And somehow I knew you would be here."

His mouth went dry, and there was a peculiar ache in his chest he was unable to identify. "I was afraid I'd hurt you or scared you." It was as he said it that he finally understood some of the desperation that had been urging him to find her again. He wanted to ensure she was well, that he hadn't petrified her with his rough tupping.

"I enjoyed every moment of our time together." Was it his imagination that her husky rasp seemed familiar?

"Were you at the ball just now?"

Silence.

"Were *you*?" came her rejoinder.

"Yes."

"So was I."

He pushed from the wall, moving to the ghostly outline. "Perhaps we danced." Somehow, he sensed her amusement. "Are you smiling?"

"Yes," she said, so softly, he strained to hear.

A hand bumped into his shoulder, then traveled down past his elbow as her fingers searched for his. When she found his hand, she took it and raised it to her mouth. There, he traced the curve of her lips.

"I'm still smiling."

Without overthinking the visceral need, he cupped her cheek and took her lips.

Sheer paradise.

She was sweet and soft and decadent. Each touch, each rough kiss, was an erotic torment. He needed her...*this*. They pulled apart breathing raggedly.

"I have so many questions," she whispered. "So many hungers. My mind has not been quiet, and somehow, I thought if I encountered you tonight, the uncertainty would be silenced. Instead, it has multiplied."

He dropped his forehead to hers. "You want to know me," Oliver said, tempted beyond measure to speak in his normal tone, and not this low, rough whisper. Except, there was a need to honor her request for anonymity. He didn't want her to think for one second he was a dishonorable bounder.

"No," she said in a fierce whisper, but there was a tremble in her voice. "I do not want us to know each other's identity," she declared, a little too emphatically.

"Let's for one moment just think—"

She stole the rest of his words in a kiss that burned all his thoughts to ashes.

"I don't want to think, or talk, not now. Only feel."

Oliver had hard sexual tastes, and it made no sense to spring any surprise on her. Their first time, he hadn't been as unrestrained as he liked. If she would be reluctant to try the kind of play he would be interested in, it was better to find out now than when he was balls deep, especially since he had been afraid he had hurt her before. "I want to fuck you long and hard for the whole night, until you can't think or speak. All the noise in your head will be drowned out."

"Show me," she taunted with a provocative arch into his

embrace.

He kissed her with such passion her lips would surely be swollen. Moving with her, he pressed her against the wall, pushing her nightgown high on her thighs.

Her subtle, delicate scent surrounded him, only this time, it was lavender.

"You wore a different scent that first night," he growled in between the almost rough kisses he placed on her lips.

"Yes…"

His thumb dragged along the soft curve of her inner thighs, and without much encouragement, she parted her legs. He trailed his fingers over the soft flesh of her buttocks and around to her mound.

He marveled at the silky feel of her skin, the wonderful taste of her tongue as she dueled with his in their incendiary kiss. He tucked two fingers at the entrance of her sheath, loving the soft flutters as she trembled in anticipation. He shoved them deep, and a moan broke low in her throat. Oliver pulled his fingers out slowly, dragging them against her walls, then thrust them deep again, driving her onto the tips of her toes.

Her soft cry at his action was husky, sultry. And it traveled straight to his cock, hardening him even more. Breaking the kiss, they took panting breaths, trading air with each other. "Your pussy is the tightest I have ever felt. When I am done with you, you will be looser, sorer, but you will enjoy every stroke I give you tonight."

A gratified groan tore from his throat as wetness bathed his fingers. He leaned in closer, so their lips were only a whisper apart. "I want you to ride my tongue before taking my cock."

Her hips rolled into him, and he rewarded her with another thrust.

"Have your legs ever been tied open and your pussy

eaten for hours with no respite from the pleasure, even if you scream for mercy?"

She jerked and gripped him tightly. "You've read more of my diary."

In her voice, he heard the duality of shame and acute pleasure. He kissed the spot beneath her ear tenderly. "Yes." Oliver had a desperate need to pleasure her in all the forbidden ways she'd ever yearned for. He wanted to wipe away the shame her husband had inspired for her wonderful sensuality. Her passion was pure and honest, dark and wanton, and he wanted her to embrace it with all the fierceness he could feel simmering inside.

She leaned forward and took his lips in a raw, carnal kiss. Her aggression surprised him, aroused him, and captivated the dark needs flowering in his soul. She took control of the kiss, all but climbing his hand to wrap her legs around his waist.

His hand smoothed over the rounded cheeks of her ass. "I want to take you on a darker journey of sexuality."

Her voice was dark, heavy with lust. "I'm willing to go wherever with you, my lord."

The knowledge that she might very well do so had his pulse jumping in his throat and lust stroking over his aching cock. The idea that he could explore all his desires with this woman was thrilling and terrifying. It was also a risk—he could either enthrall or repulse her.

He ran his fingers down the shadowy cleft of her rear. "I'm going to sink my cock here…"

She tensed, then her body relaxed, though only marginally. "Is that possible?"

There was no fear, or disgust, only curious hunger. Oliver's knees felt weak. Who was she to be so fearless with her burgeoning passions? "Yes."

"And I'll feel pleasure?"

He allowed his fingers to linger over the curves of her rear as he leaned close to plant a soft kiss between her shoulder blades. "I'll burn you alive with it," he promised hoarsely. "I also want to fuck your mouth, feel these lips sucking and pleasuring me with tight, hot pulls."

"Yes."

Oliver sank to his knees and pressed a kiss to the top of her bare mound, inhaling the sweet muskiness of her arousal. He'd never had a lover be so willing to burn in illicit passion with him before. Of course, the women of the brothels he'd visited had been willing to do anything for a coin...but none of his mistresses or lovers had granted him such trust.

He would not betray that confidence and vowed she would enjoy every moment of their tryst. He slowly stood and lowered her nightgown. Then he intertwined their fingers and brought their clasped hands to his lips, where he brushed a fleeting kiss across her knuckles.

Then he tugged her along the corridor, toward the promise of bliss. And she followed without asking any questions, the soft padding of her feet implying she was also barefoot. The level of her faith humbled him, beguiled him, and left him wondering how it was possible to feel such depth of emotion for a woman he had never seen.

Chapter Nine

Her lover's voice was dark, edgy, and it had wicked lust uncurling in the pit of her stomach. Need whipped like lightning through her bloodstream, heating her body so that every one of Lily's nerve endings pulsed with fire at his words. What he threatened to do to her was hedonistic—but she wanted it, him, in every way. The thrill of being so *improper* and free had her arousal spiking higher, and her breath came in short pants. It didn't feel unsavory…instead it felt right and perfect.

She was grateful she wasn't quaking with nerves. Except, with each step, her knees weakened. Where was he taking her? He paused, and then she heard several clicks before, with a whoosh, another portal opened into what appeared to be a bedchamber. Lily hovered on the threshold, staring into a room covered in shadows and slashes of silvery moonbeams. Lemon wax was redolent in the air, an indication the space had been recently cleaned. There was a large canopied bed, the white curtains over the bed a beacon. "You anticipated my presence."

"I believe it was more of a prayer. I had this room prepared after the first time I encountered you. We are on one of the upper floors of the west wing. No other chambers are occupied on this floor, so there will be no chance of anyone overhearing us."

"You must have been charmingly persuasive for the marquess's housekeeper to prepare this room. Mrs. Wright is frightfully proper and would certainly deduce your intentions."

A low grunt was his only reply, and Lily smiled. Inexplicably, she hesitated in moving into the room. He did not prod her forward but simply waited, and she recalled he had shown a similar restraint at their first encounter. He clearly didn't believe in using force. "You are different from the men I've known."

The confession lay between them, and she closed her eyes, cursing silently.

"Do you speak of your husband?"

One of them. Lily swallowed. "Yes."

She jerked slightly as he rested his hand on her lower back. His soft touch was reassuring instead of intimidating. Acting on an unknown instinct, she leaned back into him, the top of her forehead gently butting his chin. "You're patient and kind."

She felt him assessing her words.

"And he wasn't?"

The memories of the few times the vicar had rushed into her body without preparing her rose inside her. "No, he wasn't."

"I'm sorry," he said gruffly. "He was a buffoon."

She smiled. "The memory barely stings. My husband only made it to my bed a handful of times."

It was the way he had screamed at her afterward and shamed her for making him lose control that still burned her soul. Vicar Layton had thought it a sin to feel lust for his young wife, and he had blamed her for her sensuality, so much so she had tried her best to dress modestly so as not to tempt him. The hours of prayers afterward on their knees in the rectory had been exhausting. Though she had earnestly prayed for her desires to vanish, the sense of being unfulfilled had only grown stronger. *Harlot...Jezebel.* She bit into the soft of her lip, hating that those hurtful words would echo in her heart at this moment.

"Are you married?" she whispered.

He stiffened. "I would never dishonor my wife by being here with you."

"Is that a no or a deflection?"

Rough amusement coated the voice that replied, "That is a definite no."

"A mistress?"

"No."

"Are you disfigured in some manner?"

His low laugh caressed her ear. "No."

"Then why are you here...*now.*" For she truly did not understand it. "These are questions I should have asked when we first met, but I was too caught up in the excitement and impropriety of it all."

"I am here because I had hoped that you would be."

So simple, yet so complicated. Who was he? Anonymity was her rule, but she was desperate to know who this man in the darkness was. Lily shook away the feeling. This must only be an indulgence in pleasure and the only need she should possess. The feelings that had been burgeoning in her heart as she danced with the marquess had been too frightening. She had all but asked him to paint her in the nude. *Dear God.* And then in the library when he'd started painting her... oh, the swirls of wants and needs long denied had rushed through her with crippling intensity. It would be foolish to allow herself to fall for a man so above her in circumstances and expectations. She wanted to drown her thoughts under the sharp lash of pleasure this stranger had invited her to ride on a few days past.

Releasing the doubts, she glided into the room, her feet sinking into plush carpets.

"Would you like a drink? There's wine and brandy."

"No. I only need you."

She barely made out the outline of the man who clasped her hips and turned her to face him. His lips touched hers with a soft, sweet possession that made her heart trembled. She parted her lips, and his tongue swept inside. He teased her with shallow strokes, before biting down on her bottom lip. She gasped at the sensuous sting, and he swallowed it, kissing her hard, wet, and deep.

The hands that peeled off her nightgown did so slowly, and then his fingers ran over her body, caressing her dips and curves with sensual dominance.

"How I wish I could see these delightful curves." He lifted her, and a few strides later, her world shifted, then cool silken sheets met her body. As he bore her back to the bed, his lips caught hers again in a passionate kiss. He released her mouth, and firm hands pushed her knees up and then out in a lascivious sprawl.

The sudden sweet, stabbing invasion of his tongue in the tender folds of her pussy had her gasping. Somehow, he rolled with her so that she was sitting astride his face. Shock and uncertainty unbalanced her momentarily, but he gripped her hips, steadying her, and then raked his tongue over her aching clitoris.

His words came back to her. *I want you to ride my tongue before taking my cock.* How splendidly wicked. Lily grabbed the headboard and rolled her hips, gasping at the blast of pure pleasure that tore through her. Though it was his lips and tongue, she was in control of how sweet and how blisteringly hot the pleasure she felt could get.

Her thighs trembled, he groaned, and she undulated.

Oh, there!

He latched on to her nub and sucked. Lily screamed. Unable to help the fevered need blooming through her, she opened her thighs a little wider, arched her hips, and rode her lover's face. His wicked tongue brought her to the edge without tipping her over. She sobbed, grinding faster on his diabolical tongue, desperate to feel that intense pleasure once more. He gripped her buttocks and positioned her slightly differently, and then drove his tongue into her.

She convulsed, ecstasy bowing her back, and she bucked against his mouth as sensations raced through her. As if he were terribly impatient for her, a few seconds later, she found herself flipped to her stomach and drawn up to her knees. She collapsed to her elbows, feeling her entire body blush at the lascivious way she was open to him. He settled behind her, his cock probing her entrance. When he pushed forward, her muscles burned at the tight impalement. A wild cry tore from her throat as, with three heavy thrusts, he buried his length deep inside of her.

"*Yes*," she cried out brokenly.

She trembled on him, feeling impaled but craving more. "Oh, please," she moaned. "Make me burn...harder."

"Slow and easy." His fingers tightened on her hips. His touch was warm, reassuring, and felt so right. "I want you to feel every inch of my cock stretching your tight, sweet cunt."

Oh God, it was better than she had ever thought it could be.

His body slid into hers with sensual power as he fucked into her over and over with pure male greed and lust, drawing Lily into a maelstrom of exquisite sensations. He was not gentle. He took and took, drowning her in a sea of pleasure-pain as he rode her hard. A tight heat formed in her core, growing tauter with every lunge of his powerful body. Lily screamed into the sheets, twisting them as his hips snapped deeper, splintering the pleasure that had coiled so tightly inside of her.

Her muscles clamped down too tightly on his still thrusting cock, creating a friction that had her sobbing in his arms. He stretched her limits, her endurance, and what she thought she knew of loving. She hurt, but it was such a sweet pain, and she was so wet that smacking noises reverberated in the air, and the sound of skin sliding against damp skin filled the darkened room.

Later, she would probably look back and embarrassment would strike her, but for now, she was a creature of pure sensation, riding the dark, erotic edge of pleasure and pain as the heavy width of his cock pounded into her, pleasure obliterating all sense of decorum and any modesty she'd once possessed. A strangled cry tore from her throat as pleasure seared her body. He rode her through the storm of exquisite sensations, and then with a heavy groan, he emptied his seed deep inside her shivering body.

She collapsed, and he tumbled with her, but turned so that she was splayed on top of his muscled chest. Most of the moon had vanished behind the clouds, and a cool air wafted through the room, shifting the heavy draped.

Who are you? she desperately wanted to ask. Did his face tighten with pleasure, the corded muscles of his throat held taut when he took his release? What did her lover's eyes look like when he released his seed into her body? What color were his eyes...the shape of his lips? When she felt his smile against her hair...what did it look like? Were they firm... sensually cruel or sweet and boyish? Lifting her hands, she allowed her fingers to ghost over his lips. The filthy, erotic words he had used to rouse the wanton creature in her, and the way he had licked her pussy and pushed her to climax with such delight said these lips were sensually cruel.

Was he Lord Bolton, Mr. Darwhimple, Viscount Milton…? Perhaps Lord Ambrose?

Her heart kicked as images of the marquess filled her thoughts. He had been so dark and dashingly elegant as he twirled her around the ballroom tonight. All the young ladies had glared at her with envy and disbelief…and the marchioness had been unable to mask her disapproval. Lily would face an inquiry in the morning, and she would have to reassure Lady Ambrose her son had only been kind.

Or was her lover Mr. Braddock or Viscount Hardwick?

A knot of emotion clogged her throat. How could two people be so soul-shatteringly intimate, yet might pass in the corridor a few hours from now and not know each other? She fought the need to curl into his arms. Lily was falling in too deep with a stranger. A ridiculous notion, but what else could account for the needs awakening in her soul?

Her lover smoothed his hand over the globes of her buttocks, up to the curves of her stomach.

"I've released my seed inside you."

She sucked in a sharp breath. Was he worried about foisting a bastard on her? She pushed aside the ache building in her chest. Lily could not bring herself to explain why he worried for naught.

"If there are consequences from our passions, you will need to know who I am."

She stiffened. "Is this your way of trying to uncover my identity?"

"No," he murmured. "It is a credible concern."

Lily frowned, thinking swiftly. It was not common knowledge that she was unable to bear fruit. Perhaps to reveal her state would not be a clue to her identity. Still, she hesitated, a peculiar feeling of vulnerability creeping over her. She frantically thought of the things she had learned from reading salacious books like *Fanny Hill*. "I...I am a woman of the world. I've taken precautions."

"Such as?" Incredulity rang in his tone.

"I'm sure you are a man of the world yourself and know of which I speak."

"Educate me," he murmured drily.

Lily swallowed, grateful they were in the dark because she was blushing. "I inserted a small sponge with vinegar."

His grunt revealed he had indeed heard of such practices to prevent conception. "Curious. All I tasted was the sweetness of your cunt."

The heat in her face multiplied.

"Are you by chance blushing?"

"Of course not," she gritted out.

A low chuckle came from him. Her lover eased her gently off his body and pushed from the bed. He padded over to the window, where the moonlight painted a section of his body in a silvery glow. She came up on her elbows, her heart a pounding mess, wondering if the light would illuminate his face. There was a splash of water, and she made out that a basin was on a small table. Her lover turned around, and she gasped audibly. His body was a work of art. His chest and arms flexed with power, his tight abdomen rippled with strength. And his manhood...*dear heavens*. Though flaccid, it hung heavy and thick. Now she understood the ache her core throbbed with even now.

He stepped forward, and the darkness swallowed him once more. His weight dipped the bed. "Open your legs."

She complied. Fingers stroked up her legs to her tender core. Then something damp and cool replaced his questing fingers. He touched her with exquisite gentleness as he cleaned their combined release from her body.

"Tell me your name."

She flinched at the unexpected request. "No," she said, careful to keep her tone low and husky.

"Do you wonder who I am?"

Always. "Yes."

"I hunger to know you."

"You are in possession of my diary, which holds my most secret thoughts."

He gripped her hips and encouraged her to turn and lay on her stomach in the center of the large bed. Then he used the washcloth and cleaned the hollow between her buttocks. Her eyes widened when he lingered a little too long at that forbidden entrance. The cloth disappeared, and a few seconds later, the heat of him blanketed her body. He was careful to keep most of his weight off her, and Lily felt perplexing reassured and intimidated in equal measure by his muscled hardness.

"Your words reveal to me your wanton heart, but there is so much more, isn't there?"

A fierce joy clutched at her heart that he wanted to know more about her. She also wept with relief, for she had a similar need, and it felt incredible to know he didn't just see her as a quick, nameless liaison.

"What is the dance you like best?"

"The waltz." The only time she had ever indulged in the scandalous dance was earlier with Lord Ambrose. How delightful it had been. "I feel so free and alive when I am twirled across the ballroom floor."

He pressed a light kiss on her shoulder. "Do you like animals?"

What a curious question. "Some," she admitted. "Mostly dogs and birds. You, my lord?"

"Horses and dogs, I enjoy immensely. Which bird?"

"The canary is my favorite."

His lips curved into a smile. "Children?"

"Oh, yes, there is nothing more precious."

"Do you have any?"

Tension thrummed through her veins. "No."

Soft, soothing kisses danced around her neck and shoulders.

"What is your favorite color?"

"Yellow. It reminds me of sunshine and happiness."

"I like blue because it reminds me... I am flummoxed as to why, but I enjoy the color and the various shades presented as blue."

She laughed.

"Are your eyes blue by any chance?"

"Brown."

"Another delightful hue."

Lily gasped. "You sneaky scoundrel!"

"You wound me, my sweet. I simply want to know you. I do not believe anything will ever equal the perfection of tasting your lips, of inhaling your moans and cries, feeling your wetness coating my fingers, of tasting the sweetness of your pussy. *No one.* With such a revelation, surely, I must know who you are?"

She moaned at the forbidden pictures his illicit words created in her mind.

As if unable to help himself, he bent and pressed a kiss at the curve of her hip and dragged his lips to the rounded globes of her derriere and bit...hard, then licked to soothe the sting.

"I love the soft feel of your skin under my tongue. You taste like cherries."

Lily giggled, enjoying the sweet heat building in her veins.

"Tell me your name," he coaxed, whispering kisses over her buttocks and hips.

"No."

"Why ever not?"

"Because if we know each other, *this* will have to end before the conclusion of Lady Ambrose's house party. We have two more days...let us enjoy them."

"And if my intentions are honorable?"

She twisted her head and stared at his dark outline in ill-concealed shock. "What do you mean?"

"I would like to court you."

"I beg your pardon?"

"You heard me, my lady."

Lily felt faint. "Upon my word, surely you are jesting."

"No," he murmured. "Are you married, or promised to another?"

"Of course not!"

"Ill-formed in some manner?"

The dratted man was turning her questions on her. "No."

"We are suited in many ways."

"Only between the sheets," she snapped. "You have no notions of my connections or reputation."

"So, inform me," he rebutted lightly.

The low, rough dulcets had evened out into a smooth, clipped, but lushly sensual accent, quite reminiscent of the voice she imagined in her ears whenever she pleasured herself.

It was the voice of her nighttime fantasies and provocative dreams.

Panic crashed into her senses with the weight of a boulder. She tensed against her lover, and her fingers dug into his forearm. "You are no longer disguising your voice," Lily said weakly. What had changed?

His breath caressed her ear. "Picked up on that did you?"

There it was again; it was undoubtedly *him*. "I... Good heavens," she stammered. "Lord Ambrose?"

"At your service, my lady."

Her head spun as if she was tippled. Sweet mercy. This

was impossible. The marquess was her midnight lover. So many emotions jumbled through her—apprehension, guilt, triumph, pleasure, relief—and she was unable to halt the onslaught. There was a place in her heart where she hid dreams and impossible yearning. It cracked open, and the sweetest feeling of delight filled her. The most sought-after bachelor of the season, Lord Oliver Carlyle, the Marquess of Ambrose, powerful, charming, and kind, distressingly handsome, was her lover. *And let's not forget indecently rich.*

They had held so many conversations this week. *Dear God.* "Do you have any notion of my identity?" she asked tentatively, careful to ensure her voice remained low and husky.

"I know who you are not."

"I do not gather your meaning."

"There are five widows in attendance. Viscountess Falconbridge, Mrs. Maryann Elliot, Mrs. Eleanor Bainbridge, Lady Henrietta, and the Dowager Countess of Melbourne. Which one are you? I am certain you are not Mrs. Elliot or Viscountess Falconbridge since you have no child."

Lily's heart stuttered with relief and troubling disappointment. Of course he would only consider the women his mother had invited to Belgrave Manor, not a widowed servant living under his nose. *Dear heavens.* That was why he had danced with Mrs. Elliot and Lady Henrietta earlier, and why he would court widows. The wretched man had been trying to find her. The notion of his mother's paid companion being his notorious lover hadn't occurred to him. It hurt, for it implied he had no thought of her beyond their easy banter and his charitable offer of money for little or no service.

It would have been wonderful to know a man like the marquess could desire her. A fierce stab of guilt pierced her. If he knew he lay with a servant, surely his noble senses would be offended. She would probably be relieved of her position before the month's notice she had been given. How would he bear to look at her, to see her in his house by his mother's side, if he knew he had lowered himself so?

"Well?"

She twisted around in the cage of his arms so that his heavy body was now cradled between her thighs. Despite the leaden weight in her chest, she wrapped her arms around his shoulders and pressed a wet, open-mouthed kiss in the hollow of his throat.

"Don't," he groaned. "Do not distract me from my purpose, you wicked minx."

It *was* a distraction, but she couldn't face any more questions or dwell too long on the tangle of emotions in which she was currently caught. Lily was truly at a loss that the man she was falling hopelessly in love with was the same man she had admired for so long. A man that she could never hope to have a future with.

"My lord," she whispered.

"Yes?"

When she spoke, her voice cracked with emotion. "Call me Dahlia."

He stiffened. "Is that your name?"

"One of them." Her father was a botanist, and the names he bestowed on his children reflected his love and passion for flowering plants. She could only pray her marquess would not connect Lily with Dahlia, but she wanted to hear one of her names whispered from his lips when he found his pleasure.

She rolled her hips below him, and at the same time nipped the underside of his jaw. "Fuck me."

He chuckled, the soft sound holding such sensual menace she purred.

"You cannot take more of me at this moment...Dahlia." He kissed the corner of her mouth. "This is not the way to distract me, *that* I promise you."

He was perhaps correct in his assessment, her core still felt very tender, but the promise of tormenting pleasure in his soft warning had arousal stirring in her veins. She reached down between them and fisted his manhood, which was already rising hard and sure. Twisting her wrist, she stroked up and down, gratified at the deep rumble that pulsed from his throat.

Everything felt more acute, knowing that the man above her was Oliver. How she wished she could grant him a similar delight, if only he wouldn't possibly turn from her in disgust. Arching her hips, she wrapped her legs around his back, her heels digging into his firm buttocks. Then she rubbed the tip of his length over her aching nub. Lily's entire body burned under the lash of pleasure.

"Where have you been all my life?" he whispered, making her heart leap.

She got so wet, so fast, as she rubbed him in circles, trembling at the sensations quaking through her. She should be mortified at the ease at which her sex was soaked with her arousal. The wretched man did not help her, only holding himself still, his forearms braced above her head locked with tension.

With a muttered curse, he fisted his cock, pushed it against her opening, and shoved to the hilt. She cried out, distantly hearing his groan, *Dahlia* a rough entreaty on his lips. He paused to take her hands and draw the curtains attached to the canopied bed, firmly binding her hands with the silk. Lily tugged at the restraints, a weak, hungry sensation flowering through her.

"I want my name on your lips," he ordered, shoving his cock deep into her in one smooth stroke. For an instant, they both lay unmoving at the exquisite fit.

"Oliver," she instantly breathed.

Wet heat trailed at her neck, his teeth nipping and delivering sharp stings. One of his hands slipped between them, down to her mound, to pinch her sensitive nub. She jerked under the sharp lash of sensation. Her wail echoed in the dark chamber as he started to ride with shocking depth and strength. His devilish finger stroked her throbbing clitoris while his hips surged into her with erotic power, sinking her deep into the mattress as he ravaged her.

The friction of his thumb against her clitoris as he rubbed it hard, and his rough pounding, had Lily biting into the muscles of his shoulder, her pussy quivering helplessly around his almost punishing thrusts. Raw, piercing sensation filled her, and Oliver overwhelmed her senses with a pleasure so brutal, Lily arched her neck and screamed his name as shards of ecstasy consumed her.

"I need more of you," he groaned, his breath feathering over her damp forehead.

"Yes," she sobbed, caught between wanting to rest and drowning in flames of delight once more. Sharp bursts of pleasure sizzled along her nerve endings as Lily responded to his urgings with flaming sensuality. There was enough length on her silken restraints for her to loop her bound hand around his neck and pull his lips to her. Oliver pressed their mouths together in a hungry kiss, his tongue teasing and plundering her mouth as he rode them to fulfillment.

Chapter Ten

An hour after she had slipped from the chamber and hurried through the secret passages, Lily groaned as she sank into the heated depths of a bathtub. She had fretted she would be discovered as she'd furtively heated the water in the kitchen and lugged it up the stairs to her large copper tub in her bath chamber. Her muscles had protested, but she had marshaled on without rousing any of the other servants until her bath had been ready. A sigh of pleasure escaped her lips as the water soothed the aches and pain in her body. Though the tender ache in her core would last for days, she wouldn't trade her experience for anything, for now she would have several memories to cherish when the nights were cold and lonely.

A face to picture, and a deep, masculine, and achingly sensual voice to remember.

What would he have to recall? Her throat tightened, and tears splashed her cheeks, the salt stinging her bruised lips.

How delightfully thorough he had been as he had debauched her at least twice more before they had fallen into a slumber. She had eased his arm from her waist, slithered from the bed, and donned her nightgown as quickly as possible before fleeing. Under no circumstances could she see him again. To think she had been silly enough to entertain the notion of something more lasting, like an affair. The marquess was hunting for a bride, one who had impeccable connections and who could give him children. Any of the widows in attendance could give him that, along with the added benefit of being a woman of experience.

Lily refused to linger over impossible dreams—she had dreamed enough of those over the last eight years. Only her shop and building her clientele needed her attention.

. . .

The very next morning was dreary. The clouds were dark, and rain hovered on the horizon. Lily had still ventured outside for her morning walk and to also escape the discontented guests in the drawing rooms and music room. They most certainly believed grumbling about the weather was warranted, and she had wanted to escape it.

A gust of wind tried to tug the bonnet from her head, whipping her pale-yellow day dress high around her legs. With a scowl at the sky, she turned around and hurried back to the manor. Perhaps she had lingered too long and most certainly had strolled too far. She had taken the path that led to the village, and Belgrave Manor could not be seen from where she stood.

"Mrs. Layton…Lily?"

She whirled around and slipped, cursing when she tumbled. The marquess lunged and grabbed her, steadying her with strong arms.

"It seems as if all I do around you is trip, my lord."

"I startled you, forgive me."

She pulled from the clasp that still lingered. "Forgiven."

It took an inordinate amount of strength to contain her blush when she peered up at him. Did he truly not know she was his lover? She assessed him from beneath her lashes. The marquess did not look at her as if he had ravished her for hours last night. "I...I was taking a walk, but the weather has forced me back to the manor."

He glanced over his lands in the direction of Belgrave manor.

"I, too, desired a stroll. It seems we are both restless and disenchanted with the house party. Our hunting lodge is close by. We could wait out the impending squall there." He rested a palm on his chest and gave her a charming smile. "I swear on my honor, I will be the soul of politeness and discretion."

"You always are, my lord." Except for when he had taken her last night. That man had been raw and untamed. The blush she had been fighting rushed through her cheeks and flushed along her entire body. It would be prudent to go with him, for to proceed back to the main estate would see her caught in the downpour. She felt light-headed and hopelessly uncertain how to behave. The only thing she was sure of was that she couldn't be enclosed with him in a confined space again.

"Are you well, Lily?" Those beautiful eyes were dissecting every nuance of her expression with a puzzled frown.

"Oh yes, I'm quite well. Just a slight headache."

Unable to help herself she lowered her eyes to his firm, sensual mouth. She had kissed those lips, tangled her tongue with his, and dear God, the memory of what that wicked mouth had done to her pussy had unbearable heat twisting through her veins.

"My mother seems quite taken with Viscount Clayton. I doubt she will need you today. You do look tuckered—why don't you take the day and rest?"

The Marquess of Ambrose was deliciously intriguing.

The scoundrel and the gentleman. The two were melded into a beautifully appealing—but so dangerous—indistinguishable whole.

How courteous and gentlemanlike he had been on their walk.

Permit me to help you over the log.

Then last night…

Even though the darkness is a forbidden delight, I long to see you…and the pink folds of your cunt glistening with your need.

And he wanted to court her. *No…not me,* she reminded herself sternly. He wanted to court his adventurous and mysterious lover, the bold and lustful Lady Dahlia, not Mrs. Lily Layton, passably pretty, too rounded, no money or connection…and barren. No distinction that could recommend her to the role of a marchioness. She needed to remove the ache and want his words had placed in her heart.

"Lily?"

She struggled to recall his previous question. "The fresh, cold air will set me right, but I thank you for thinking of me."

His gloriously wicked mouth curved into a small smile. "We could return to the manor and you sit for me."

There was a watchful air about him that set her heart to pounding. "I…I do not believe it wise for me to pose today." How could she sit for him in intimate seclusion knowing he was her lover? Surely, she would give herself away with her blushes. Last night in the library she had been filled with such indelible awareness—her breathing had been too fast, and the flesh between her legs had been slick with need. And she hadn't known, then, he was her secret lover. Surely her reaction would be more unpardonable now.

Something heated and dark flashed in his eyes before his expression shuttered. "Perhaps in a few days," he murmured, his penetrating stare assessing every nuance of her face.

"Yes." She took a small, steady breath. "Please, go on without me."

"Of course," he said with a dip of his head. "Have a pleasant walk."

Then he sauntered in the opposite direction, without looking back. She watched him go, the most peculiar, desperate sort of ache working through her heart. *If only...*

She squeezed her eyes to banish the foolish dreams she would not allow to take root.

It would be foolish of her to venture into the secret passageway again. Now that he had revealed himself, he would be much more determined to uncover her identity. He thought her a woman of his society, that he could woo her. Were he to discover that he had been bedding a woman so far below him... Would he truly be disgusted? Would he remove his offer to pay her? The notion did not feel at all right to Lily. The marquess seemed too kind and honorable, but she couldn't take the chance. She would simply treasure all the forbidden encounters from that wanton, secret place in her heart.

It had been truly glorious, and she would not have traded the past nights for anything, but she had to be strong and avoid the marquess—and his wicked tongue, fingers, and cock.

• • •

Lily Layton laughed, her head thrown back, her neck arched quite delightfully, her eyes filled with enjoyment. The sun struck her just right, and there was an indefinable sensation filling Oliver's heart as he stared at her through his studio window two stories up. She sat with the other servants under a large oak tree, having some sort of picnic. Everyone had been thrilled when the sun had broken through the clouds, and had hurried outside to bask in the pale rays.

His fingers and paintbrush moved as if they had a life of their own, and Lily slowly appeared on his canvas. Oliver shifted closer to the window, pressing his nose to the cold glass pane. *There…sweet Christ.* That angle was just perfect.

He lost himself, painting the curve of her lips, the slope of her jaw, the arch of her neck. Suddenly he could imagine her…spread-eagle on his crisp white sheets, splayed wide and bound by silk as he spanked the wet folds of her cunt.

Oliver dropped the brush and raked his fingers through his hair, uncaring that he would transfer paint to his hair. Somehow, his fevered fantasy and desperate hope had conjured the idea that his mysterious lover and Lily Layton were the same. The image was evocative and vivid, down to the vibrant red of her hair, the high thrusting breast, and golden-brown eyes wide with pleasure and apprehension.

Mrs. Lily Layton…and Dahlia. The very notion was ridiculous, or perhaps he wanted Lily so badly he imagined that a demur and respectable lady like her could be so wanton. Was it possible two different women could so captivate him?

Moving to the small table near his easel, he picked up the diary. The hunger in his heart to know both women was driving him mad.

Dearest Diary,

I had cake for breakfast. Three wonderful slices. I even licked the icing from my fingers, quite unladylike, I know, but it was glorious. I believe I shall have cake again at luncheon.

Oliver smiled, fancying he could feel the defiant joy in that simple statement. Devil take it. He wanted his secret lover and Mrs. Lily Layton to be the same, despite its impossibility. With a curse, he snapped the journal closed, put it back on the table, and exited the room, moving down the corridors then the winding staircase at a quick pace.

"Branson, where is my mother?" Oliver asked the butler.

"Her ladyship is taking tea in the Rose drawing room, my lord."

Grateful he wouldn't have to search Belgrave Manor and possibly find her in a compromising situation with the viscount, Oliver made his way to the drawing room. Despite what his mother thought, he wasn't oblivious to her liaison with the much younger viscount. If Oliver recalled correctly, the man was at least ten years her junior. But he would not interfere, not when his mother seemed so happy for the first time in years.

He entered the drawing room, his gaze settling on his mother. She was alone, busy writing by the windows overlooking the gardens she tended herself.

"Mother."

She glanced up with a warm smile. "Oliver! I missed you at breakfast…and luncheon. Oh, I see, you've been painting. You are a mess," she said, giving a delicate sniff.

Dahlia had exhausted him, and he had been mildly surprised to wake and find her gone. "I overslept, and then I went on a long ride to clear my thoughts."

His mother frowned and gently put down her quill. "Is everything quite well, my dear?"

"Yes."

"Are you here to discuss Lady Emma?"

"No, Mother. Vicar Layton."

She frowned. "What about him?"

"Would you confirm his Christian name, please?"

"I believe it was Robert."

Oliver contained his reaction, though his heart wanted to burst from his chest. Robert had been the name in the diary. Lily Layton and his mysterious stranger were one and the same. "Thank you."

"What is that about?"

"Nothing of import, please return to your writing."

The marchioness harrumphed and once more dipped her quill into the ink pot.

Oliver scrubbed a hand over his face. With all the examination he had done of widows, he had never thought... never in his wildest imagination had he thought to consider the widow who had been living under his roof for months.

He left the Rose drawing room then headed to his chamber and called for a bath. The evidence was still flimsy at best, but what were the chances of two widows' departed husbands being called Robert. And it hadn't been Oliver's imagination that she had behaved oddly this morning. She had stared and acted so flustered. She had seemed different today, and there had been knowledge, and also something heated and elusive, whenever he met her regard.

Impossible...yet probable.

A groan whispered past his lips. Dahlia could only be Lily Layton. Had he unwittingly bedded an employee in his household? The even more distressing realization was that he wanted to do it again, and again.

He shrugged from his jacket, removed his waistcoat, and slowly unbuttoned his shirt. This bore further investigation. He would clean the paint from his body, dress, and return downstairs to mingle with his guests before going over the investment portfolio his banker had sent down this morning. Then, after dinner, he would wait a reasonable time then venture into the secret passages.

Only this time, he would take the one that led to Lily Layton's bedchamber.

Several hours later, Oliver felt like an ass, standing at the threshold of Lily's room. He lifted his hand to draw back the portal that would show him the entrance, yet he hesitated. What if he was wrong, and he intruded on her privacy for no bloody reason? The dark voyeur in him stirred, the need twisting through him, suppressing the doubts.

He slipped open the portal and stepped closer, so he would have the perfect view. Oliver's knees almost buckled, and he braced his forearms against the wall.

Lily lay on her back, her head arched on the pillow, breasts swollen and hard, her thighs opened, her slender fingers moving desperately over the slick folds of her pussy. Her voluptuous beauty screamed of wicked nights and sultry mornings, and he allowed his eyes to devour every silken curve the soft light bathed in a warm glow.

"Oliver," she whispered.

It was a sigh of regret, of longing, and his mouth went dry at the echo of need in it. She spread her legs farther and stroked her swollen clitoris. Oliver's jaw clenched, and the hunger that coiled in his gut shocked him. He bit back the groan of need as she whispered his name again before stiffening with a cry of delight. His heart nearly exploded from his chest. Yet this was not proof that Lily was his mysterious lover, only that she pleasured herself when the need overtook her.

Relief almost made him sag.

Thank Christ. Lily Layton wanted him with the same visceral intensity with which he wanted her. It truly seemed impossible that he would desire a separate woman with the same chaotic hunger. And what if she was? He slid the portal closed and leaned against the cool wall. He'd unwittingly bedded a worker in his household after vowing never to act in any manner reminiscent of his father's proclivities. He wasn't foolish to believe he was just like his father, who had used his rank to take advantage of several servants within his household with his wife only a few rooms away. Oliver assessed the facts, recalling every minute detail of his encounters with Dahlia, and concluded that every filthy thing he had done with her delightful body, she had wanted. There had been no coercion on his part, and she certainly hadn't thought so, or she wouldn't have returned.

He closed his eyes briefly in relief. Could Lily Layton be his lover in the dark? And if she was, what would he do about it? Oliver pinched the bridge of his nose and bit back a savage curse. He was getting ahead of himself. The pressing question to be answered was whether Lily and Dahlia were truly one person. There was only one way to find out. But he wouldn't act the bumbling fool and intrude upon her now. He would be patient, and observant, and when the time was right...

God, Oliver hoped he wasn't making a mistake, and hoped he wasn't being a damn fool in planning to confront her and rip away the anonymity she'd desired.

Chapter Eleven

Lily lay in the dark, unable to sleep. For the last days and nights, she had avoided the marquess at all costs. Though she had been so very tempted to allow another encounter, she had restrained herself with a will she hadn't realized she possessed. Except now she was filled with regret, for she had lost the opportunity to have one last wicked tryst. The house party was over, and throughout the day, all the guests had departed to Town. Even Lady Ambrose had taken herself off to Bath, not too discreetly, for she traveled in the same carriage as her viscount. The large manor house was empty... save for Lily and the marquess.

If she stepped into the secret passages tonight, that would be owning up to her identity. All her feminine instincts said he would be there, despite all the guests having left. Or perhaps she was just being silly. What reason would he have to roam those corridors? It was distressing to know their *affaire de coeur*, or whatever their nightly assignations had been, were over. The pang of loss that tore through her heart was frightening.

With an irritated huff at herself, Lily pushed from the bed and tugged her robe from the peg, slipping it on over her nightgown. She moved at a sedate pace as she made her way down to the library. A solid, good book was what she needed before turning in to bed. And if that didn't work, she could also do some sketches on an idea she had for a gown.

The house echoed with emptiness, and she wondered if the marquess was still in residence. She had taken a tray into her room earlier to work on the designs for a peignoir, which was scandalously sheer. It was clear the household was abed, and as she sauntered down the hallway, she glanced at the grandfather clock near the library's entrance. It was twenty-five minutes past midnight. Though it was unlikely Oliver was up if he was in residence, she knocked on the library door and waited a few beats. When no answer came, she entered, grateful that a fire blazed and that several candles were lit, bathing the library in a warm, inviting glow.

Lily went over to the bookshelves and perused several tomes. Her fingers danced over the spines as she tilted her head, reading the titles. With a triumphant grin, she selected *The Lady of the Lake*, a book she had been longing to read.

There was a creak, and she spun around to see Oliver close the door and then lean against it. His thick hair was disheveled, and a stubble of beard shadowed his strong jaw. He was without a jacket, his cravat was loosened, and he was...he was barefoot. Something elusive pooled in the gaze that regarded her. He had never looked at her like that before. As if he was captivated.

Her heart pounded with equal measures of delight and apprehension.

Don't be silly, Lily! Though at times she had caught a lingering stare from him, it was not one filled with any fleshly longing. Unless... *Dear God,* the very notion left her mouth dry and her heart trembling.

He noticed her looking at his toes and a lazy smile swept his face. "I was in the process of undressing. I assure you, my valet is even more perplexed, since I simply left my chambers."

Her smile dwindled at his intense regard. "Is everything well, my lord...Oliver?" Of course something was the matter, or he wouldn't have abandoned getting ready for bed.

"It is." He lifted a chin to the book clutched in her hand. "You are unable to sleep."

"I...yes." Alarm slithered through her when he closed the lock with a *snick*. He had never been anything but proper with her, even when his stare had said he wanted to do wicked things with her.

"My lord—"

"We are on more intimate terms, Lily."

"Oliver—"

"I know who you are."

His pronouncement crashed into her chest like a wave, drowning her senses with panic. "I am not sure I comprehend your meaning," she said with impressive calm.

He pushed off from the door and prowled over to her, darkly dangerous and imposing. His cobalt eyes pierced her with an awareness that was disturbing and electrifying. Oliver paused only a mere inch from her, the hem of her nightgown curling around his shin. His warmth surrounded her, at once soothing and perplexingly intimidating. She knew this man...carnally...and the gentleman at the heart of him. She had nothing to fear. Yet Lily felt vulnerable in a manner she had never endured before. There could be no denying the knowledge in his eyes or the thick, heavy, predatory tension that rode the air. He lifted his hand and, with painstaking slowness, removed her mobcap and every pin that held her hair together. The risk she was taking by allowing his ministrations was so enormous she couldn't contemplate it. Nor could she move away.

"For the last few nights, I've not been able to stop thinking about you, Lily Layton. In the days, you smell like lavender… but in the nights, I can smell honeysuckle wafting from your chamber. You walk in a room, and I am aware of every breath you take. You smile, and suddenly I know the sweetly sensual shape of lips in the dark are yours."

Nerves and anticipation clutched at her throat. If she possessed any wisp of rationality, she would flee from this encounter. If he thought she was Dahlia, why wasn't he disgusted at the notion? He seemed remarkably accepting of the fact that he'd been bedding a servant.

The wavy strands tumbled down her shoulders to her mid back. "Glorious," he murmured. "What are you going to do…run…or fuck me?"

The challenge in his eyes almost felled her. An overwhelming weakness quivered through her. "My lord!" she gasped, her gaze flicking to the door and back to his. "You are being improper." Oh God, why did she continue along this vein? Surely he had irrefutable proof to approach her with his suspicions.

"Ah, denial, is it?" Oliver gripped her hips and tugged her to him, almost lifting her to the tips of her toes. The dominance in his touch had the sweetest feeling throbbing between her legs.

"I know—"

She covered his lips, her fingers trembling. "Don't say it, please, my lord."

He sucked her fingers into the heated depth of his mouth, and Lily's knees buckled, and she sagged against him. With a soft cry, she reclaimed her fingers. "Oliver, there is some mistake."

The devil smiled. "The only mistake is that I should have known sooner. Against my better judgment, I hungered for Lily Layton…I should have known you were her."

He ran his lips up the side of her neck, scraping his teeth against the slight hollow. "I want to see you naked."

Her heart fluttered madly, like butterflies trapped in a bottle.

Show some decency, the vicar had roared, spittle flying from his lips the one night she had dared to leave a candle lit in anticipation of the vicar coming to their marital bed.

Her reply, *No, I want to see you, us*, had earned her a slap on her cheek and prayers on her knees begging forgiveness for her lust filled heart for days. The vicar had ignored her then, even halting his customary peck on her cheek in the morning. Her husband hadn't visited her bed in the last two years of their marriage.

"No man has ever seen me naked," she whispered, stepping a little bit closer to the edge of madness with which he seduced her.

Oliver cupped her cheeks in strong, gentle hands. "I watched you a few nights ago as you pleased yourself and moaned my name. You were so fucking beautiful, Lily. Every dip and curve of your body was a sensual delight. I would be honored if you would bare yourself to me, my sweet."

Unspeakable desires and hunger stirred in her soul.

What are we doing, Oliver? Her tongue would not loose. Instead, Lily stepped back and pushed her nightgown from her body. Lust darkened his gaze, as she was bared before him.

An approving smile touched his lips, and he stared, his expression taut and sensually intent. "I want to take your mouth, to slide my cock past those lips and feel them suck me into heaven with hot, wet pulls." He ran his fingers down the shadowed cleft of her rear. "Before the night is over, I am going to oil you and take you here."

She shivered, a delighted thrill going through her heart as the illicit and forbidden images filled her mind. "Undress for me," she said softly. "I want to see you."

Approval flared in his eyes, and the marquess removed his shirt and trousers. He was tall and so muscled, the very picture of masculine beauty and power. She almost whimpered at the spear of lust that spread to her cunny. "I've dreamed of your lips doing wicked things to me. I'm not proper, I fear, and I will never be..."

His lips shifted into a slow, upward smile. "Any sensibilities you have left will be ruined tonight, my sweet. I am not interested in proper."

A moment later, he cupped her face between his hands and kissed her with such reverent passion that Lily's heart melted, and she knew without a doubt she was in love with the Marquess of Ambrose, a terrifying truth to contemplate.

. . .

Lily stood naked in front of Oliver, a flush covering her entire body in the most delightful pink. Her eyes glistened, and there was a slight tremble in her lower lip. Her evident vulnerability had an ache settling deep inside him.

Our wives are ladies who we must treat with revered respect. They are not common strumpets. Keep it in mind, boy, and never forget it.

Ignoring the ghost of his father's whisper, Oliver trailed a finger along his lover's jawline, down to her wide, sensual lips. She had high, graceful breasts, rounded hips, and legs that would easily wrap around the high of his back and hold while he rocked his cock into her.

"I've never seen a more beautiful woman," he said, mildly surprised at the hoarseness of his voice and the heavy ache in his loin.

Her eyes widened, then a smile curved her lips. He could do so many things—kiss, her, slowly worship the underside of that delectable breast, lay her down and feast on her sweet pussy. Instead...

"Take my cock into your mouth."

Without question, she lowered herself to her knees and clasped his cock in her soft hands. She examined his organ quite thoroughly, running her fingertip over his length to the flared mushroomed head. Then she leaned in and kissed the tip.

Sweet mercy. Her tongue was timid but felt like a whip of fire on his flesh.

Her pouting lips begged to be taken, bruised, fucked. As if she knew his carnal heart, she fisted his length and slid her mouth over his cock. He fucked slowly into her mouth, holding her hair in a firm grip, groaning at the heated wet glide of her tongue. She was so damn beautiful, with her eyes darkened and her cheeks flush with lust.

She began to move her mouth on the throbbing flesh, her tongue flickering over it, killing him with pleasure.

"That's it, Lily. Suck me deep just like that." He thrust his fingers into her hair, using his grip to anchor her as he slowly worked his prick in and out of her mouth. She stared up at him, her eyes dark pools of lust...and something far warmer than he'd anticipated.

I like you...so damn much, Lily.

He flexed his hips, pushing his flesh farther into her mouth.

She moaned around his throbbing length, a whimpering, needy sound that made his body flame. He was too close to the edge, and he wanted so much for a quick release into the silken depths of her hot little mouth. His cock sprang free from her mouth, heavy and engorged. Oliver tugged her up, and as she rose, she lightly licked his thighs and up over his rippling abdomen. His hands tightened in her hair, and a rough groan broke from his throat. He arched her, pushing her breasts up to his face. Her nipples were tight rosy buds he sucked into his mouth.

Impatience tore at him, and he walked her back toward his desk, easing her down onto the surface, and splayed her wide.

Her cunt was so pretty and pink, wet with her need for him.

"Oliver," she moaned, her thighs opening wider, her hips arching to him. "I need...I need you in me."

He tucked the head of his cock into the narrow, clenching entrance to her pussy. She cried out as he stroked inside her tight sheath, deep and hard. "Watch me take you," he murmured, glancing between their bodies as he slowly withdrew from her snug depth.

She stared up at him, her eyes dazed, unfocused, her face flushed with passion, then glanced to where they were joined. Her entire body colored red, and her tongue darted to wet those pouting lips.

Oliver groaned at the carnal picture she presented sprawled wide on his desk, her cunt stretched to take his thick length, her hair tumbling across her body and brushing her distended nipples, and those sweet, swollen lips glistening.

He slid inside her, working his length slowly and easily into her so that she felt every drag of his cock against the tightness of her slit. He pulled back, watching his cock slide nearly free of her, then worked himself back to the hilt, loving the tight grip.

She whimpered, a low, desperate sound that had his cock jerking in response.

"Oliver."

"Lily."

Then incredibly she smiled, and he understood. It felt different, better, hotter, yet so much sweeter now they had knowledge of each other. Her tongue darted and wetted her lips once again. With a groan, he thrust deep, spearing into her, feeling her pussy part to envelop him in pure bliss. "Yesss," he hissed in pleasure. "Wrap your legs around my hips."

She complied, and he lifted her from the hard desk, and with a few steps, he took them to the sofa closest to the blazing fire. He braced her against the padded arm of the couch, lifted her leg, and rocked harder and heavier inside the sensitive depths of her pussy, over and over and over.

She convulsed on his cock several times, screaming her delight, and Oliver wasn't remotely satisfied. Perspiration gleamed on their bodies as he allowed himself to be swept under the dark tide of lust, fucking her long and hard, secure in the knowledge that she matched his passions perfectly.

Chapter Twelve

"Checkmate," Lily said with a grin, peeking up at Oliver from beneath her lashes. She still wanted to pinch herself, to know they were sprawled atop a large blanket spread on his library floor, playing chess and sipping brandies, naked. It was horribly wicked of her, and she loved every minute. She felt no shame in being so bare before him, and he seemed equally amused and captivated whenever he caught her staring at his muscled form. Their clothes and unmentionable garments remained scattered on the floor, and her marquess had taken several cushions from the chaise and littered the floor with them.

He knew she was his mysterious lover and there had been no condemnation. In fact, Lily believed he was quite relieved to discover Mrs. Lily Layton and the provocative Dahlia were the same. That knowledge was distressingly fascinating. He had made no mention of courtship, which tempered her intrigue, considering it was the reason he had proffered for wanting her identity. Not that she would have said yes—he deserved better—but it would have been so wonderful to know he would still want her, without a dowry and connections.

How long did they really have as lovers? The marchioness's new lady's companion would arrive at Belgrave Manor in two weeks' time. Then Lily would take herself off to town to start the wonderful journey of opening her own business. Would the marquess wish to continue their affair?

"You are a very crafty player," he said with a smile, finally ending his analysis of the board.

"That I am, my lord."

"Who taught you?"

"My papa did. He was delighted when I showed interest at a young age. I felt like I had given him a great gift because I was smart. It was as I grew older that I realized how very different and wonderful Papa is. He encouraged my learning and did not believe certain pursuits were reserved for the men of our society."

He reached for the tumbler and refilled their glasses. "He sounds like a good man."

Lily felt as if she were floating but did not protest, taking another healthy swallow of the amber liquid.

"Easy," he cautioned.

"Who taught you?"

His beautiful eyes shadowed. "My father."

"You do not like speaking of him?"

Oliver took several sips of his brandy, his gaze considering her for several seconds. "My father was quite a brilliant businessman and strategist. From the age of twelve, I was at his side, learning how to manage the estate and other investments. He was not like other lords who believed owning businesses and working to ensure those interests remain profitable were bourgeois. He was a good father to my sisters and me."

"And you have businesses outside of your lands and property?"

"Several."

"May I ask, how did he die? The marchioness never said."

A frown split her lover's brow, and a faraway look appeared in his eyes. "In his sleep."

"Oh!"

"He was in robust health and had only ever gotten a good report from the doctors when they attended him. My father complained of a headache. He went to lie down, and a few hours later when my mother went to check on him…he was gone."

"Oh, Oliver, I am so terribly sorry."

"It was years ago, Lily, and the passage of death is normal," he said flatly.

Yet there were still shadows in his eyes. "Then why do you seem so troubled, angry even?"

Lily pushed aside the chess set, uncaring when the pieces fell from the board onto the carpet. She shifted closer to her marquess, and it felt so natural to press a kiss along the strong line of his jaw. She wanted so much to comfort him, even if she hardly understood the source of his discomfort.

"We had an argument the day before he died," Oliver said gruffly. "I felt we never repaired the hurt our words caused, and then he was gone."

She leaned back, searching his shuttered expression. "One argument and heated words can't replace a lifetime of love."

"It was rather vile, and I did not temper my anger. I found him with a kitchen maid…he was tupping her, and the girl was only fourteen."

Lily gasped.

"It was my father's vice to dally with whomever he pleased, whenever he wanted, and he often turned his lascivious attention to the servants in our household, women who I believe had little choice, even if they had wanted to decline."

"They wouldn't have refused for fear of losing their position without a recommendation," Lily said.

He tipped his head back, staring at the ceiling. "And despite his proclivities, I loved him, Lily. I loved my father still."

"I think that is the best kind of love, knowing the fault of the person and still feeling such strong sentiments."

Her lover regarded her. "I like you, Lily. I'm very glad you are Dahlia, for you see, I've been having very explicit thoughts about Lily Layton and hardly knew what to do with them."

A piercing awareness blossomed through her. "You wouldn't have seduced me," she whispered. "For I'm a dependent within your household."

"Never. I would have fought the temptation with everything in me."

"And you are not angry with me?"

There was a significant pause as he considered her question. "The very opposite. I am enthralled."

Sweet pleasure burst into her heart. "Sentiments I return wholeheartedly." Yet she wondered if, after tonight, he would ever touch her again.

Ignoring the dart of anxiety, she crawled closer and pressed her lips to his and kissed this delightful man who she wished was hers. Lips fused to his, their hearts jerking in tandem, she explored the hard planes of his chest. Within seconds, her body quickened, and passion overwhelmed her.

He eased her over, his hands strong and gentle as he turned her. Wet kisses trailed along her spine as he twisted her so she lay on her stomach. A tremble of uncertainty coursed through her when he nudged her legs wider, arching her hips to his questing fingers. Her shivering grew more pronounced, and she gripped the cushions above her head as he parted the globes of her buttocks.

When his fingertip reached the curve of her buttock, her breath audibly hitched.

"I did promise to fuck you here, didn't I?"

A breath puffed from her lips, and she nodded. A ghost of a smile curved his lips, and the sensual intent in it shot a bolt of heat straight to her core. The arousal she felt scared her. It felt too dark, too needy, too desperate. She fought to control her breathing as hunger thundered through her veins. As his finger passed the tight entrance of her ass, two fingers of his other hand dipped into the soaking depths of her core. Her body rippled, and his soft laugh was one of delight as he felt her wetness.

His chest slid against her damp back as he leaned over her, nipping her neck. "Do you want this?"

She did not want half measures. She wanted to do everything to him that she had ever dreamed of doing to a lover, to be free from shame and polite expectations, to only revel in her sexuality. Her marquess awoke a wicked craving inside her core, and he did not make her feel embarrassed at her wanton needs.

"Yes..." Her answer was dredged from deep inside of her, and she trembled at the heat that filled her. It burned away her uncertainty, her fear, and she welcomed the dark desire that flowered inside of her.

He pushed her shoulders flat to the ground and raised her buttocks for his exploration. She had never been touched there, not even by her own hands when she brought herself to pleasure. Something warm and oily glided from his fingers around her forbidden entrance, and tension sifted along her frame. Despite her wild arousal, nerves coiled inside.

A long finger slipped into her tightly clenched muscles. She cried out at the sensuous sting. The bite of pain did not repel her. Instead, laden heat surged through her limbs, and her clitoris pulsated in anticipation. Her fingers clenched in the blankets beneath her.

"Burn me alive, Lily," he lover murmured. He inserted a second...then a third finger, working her in a gentle screwing motion. She shivered beneath the caress, her hips arching toward that heated, dominant touch that was like fire against her flesh.

His hand smoothed over her hip and down the curve of her ass to her thigh. "I've hungered for a lover who would take me with such trust...with such fire as you, my sweet."

She trembled as emotions ripped through her. *And I've longed for you, too...*

Her breasts ached for relief, sensitive to the slightest of caresses of the blankets beneath her. She felt heated and sensual as he stroked her for long minutes, his fingers stretching her, preparing her, making her crazy. Lily relaxed, accepting the dark hunger and allowing the waves of pleasure to wash through her.

He shifted behind her, drawing her up onto her knees but pushing her shoulders down closer to the ground. "Arch your hips and relax."

She complied with his aroused demands.

His length flexed against her buttocks as he drew in a hard breath. She moaned, hot coils of pleasure-pain owning her as the head of his cock began to work inside her heavily oiled rear. Fire exploded along her nerves as her opening yielded increasingly under his relentless entry. She instinctively tensed. The fingers that covered her core ran over her clitoris in a lightning fast caress before thrusting deep into her pussy.

Thrill seared through her body. "Oliver," she whimpered, the lust clawing at her frighteningly.

"Relax, my sweet. You are so fucking tight, but you can take me. Push back on me and relax."

Lily forced herself to relax, to trust him, to accept the

edge of pain along with the pleasure.

"That's it," he said as she wetted his fingers. "Hold on to the cushions."

She gripped the pillows, her hips arching even more. A low moan of response broke from deep in her throat as he relentlessly pushed forward, parting her muscles with his length until he sank to the hilt. Lily wailed at the fiery pleasure-pain. She could feel him, thick and heavy, buried deep within the tightness of her body.

He pinched her clitoris and rubbed in a slow, sinuous motion as he started a gentle lunge and retreat. Her mind hazed at the shocking sensation that sizzled up her spine and had her arching in mindless want.

"You are so gorgeous...so beautiful," he whispered as he blanketed her body further with his. He pressed a kiss to her shoulder, and the fingers that had been inside her quim withdrew and stroked from her hips to the underside of her breast and up to her neck, where he encircled her throat lightly, his darker complexion an erotic contrast against her paler skin.

She whimpered, reveling in the dominance of his touch. His hand tightened around her throat ever so slightly, his thumb pressing against the fluttering pulse at the base of her neck.

"I am going to ruin you for anyone else, as you've ruined me, my sweet Lily. After tonight you will *never* think of fucking another man," he said with a hard thrust inside of her ass.

Evocative delight speared through her, dark and needy, filling her with painful splendor. Lily became a creature of pure sensation, riding the waves of sensual freedom and wildness. Her heart began to pound against her eardrums. "So, ruin me, and stop talking," she breathed out in challenge.

He vented a low, appreciative chuckle at her ear, one

filled with darkness and delight, before he nipped it with a sharp sting. His hand tightened more at her throat, and Lily barely had time to draw in a deep breath before he slammed hard and deep into her ass, with more strength than she had been prepared for. "Oliver!"

Sweat slicked her skin, she trembled, impaled on him, and a harsh sob ripped from her. The sheer domination of the act was overwhelming, and she realized Oliver was not hiding his sensuality from her. She was discovering the depths of his depraved and decadent desires.

"Your ass is choking the life from my cock...but nothing is better than your sweet cunt. Its taste, its feel, its wetness, and I can't wait to be back in your clasp."

His raw, explicit words inflamed her, and the pain of his possession gave way to dark, erotic ecstasy. Her fingers clenched on the throw cushions as he arched her ass more for his penetration. His hand remained encircling her throat, and the other gripped her hips as he worked his cock in and out of her with surging thrusts. She couldn't move, could do nothing but tremble under his weight, crying out in bliss at each penetration. A seething cauldron boiled in her. Her body tightened as bliss poured through her in torrents, a sensation pulsed from her toes to her core, eliciting an uncontrollable quivering within her thighs that soon spread to her entire body, and she orgasmed more powerfully than she thought possible.

Pleasure, like a living flame, arched over her body and burned Lily with delight. She screamed into a small cushion; she sobbed because it was too much and at the same time never enough. The rush of sensations was almost agonizing. With a guttural groan, he hugged her in a punishing grip as he emptied inside of her. Seconds passed in silence, their ragged breathing joined in a perfect symphony before he gently pulled from her.

Lily collapsed beneath him, her body still shivering with the hard aftershocks of such an exquisite climax. How would she ever be able to walk away from such pleasures?

Her lover was a comforting weight against her. He cradled her to his chest and simply held her. The warmth and contentment unfurling inside were something Lily had thought she would never know. How is it that she had been married twice and had been bereft of being held after intimacy? Her first husband had been such a sweet man, but bumbling and far too shy, and he had barely made love with her before he'd bought his commission. It had never occurred to her to cuddle up with him in their small bed. They had turned on their sides and watched each other with tentative smiles, but their young love had been too new and uncertain for them to take any further steps. Then the vicar...in the three years they had been married, they had been intimate only a handful of times, for it was sinful to lust, even in the confines of marriage.

She had never believed God despised the idea of fleshly pleasures, as the vicar had preached. After all, God had been the one to grant them such desires and lush sensuality.

Oliver moved, and she was too spent to peer back at him. She blushed as he took a warm cloth and cleaned between her tender folds and around to her bottom. With such care, she felt no discomfort, only a sense of awe.

Is he this way with all his lovers?

"How do you feel?"

Cherished. She turned her head, resting her cheek against the cushion. "Famished."

There was an uncertainty in his eyes as he peered at her, and she hardly knew how to respond to it. The marquess had always seemed so arrogant and uncompromising. Her breath hitched as she realized he waited for some reaction that would possibly wound. Was it that perhaps they were more alike than she had thought?

"I loved every minute of what just happened," she confessed softly.

Relief and approval glowed in his eyes. Lily's heart lightened. Someone had indeed been repulsed at his brand of shocking sensuality and carnal leanings. Happiness flowered inside her that she had pleased him. *How alike we are, but so far apart.*

"I cannot marry you," he said gruffly, tugging her to him. "But I need you in my life, Lily. This...whatever this is cannot end."

"I do not recall asking," she teased, pushing aside the soft ache in her heart. "I've no aspirations to be your wife. I am not ignorant of the fact that I have nothing to recommend me to the role of a marchioness." He deserved a wife that would complement his position and background, and one that would most assuredly grant him children.

"Be my mistress."

"Yes," Lily said, shocking herself.

She couldn't take back the word, for she wanted to be with him until this...whatever this was, burned out and drifted away like ashes in the wind.

Chapter Thirteen

Be my mistress.

Yes.

Lily Layton had agreed to be his mistress, yet pain had flashed in her eyes before she had shuttered her expressive gaze. Was it that she wanted more, too? A sense of disquiet pierced Oliver, for he had been longing for a more permanent connection with a lady who complimented him in all ways. His entire life he'd known the sort of woman he was duty bound to marry. Genteel, privileged, blue-blooded, with enough wealth and beauty to make any man happy. The opposite of Lily Layton. Except that everything about her was vastly appealing. A longing to have her at his side in all ways threaded through his entire body and into the depths of his soul.

If he courted her, he would be going against every expectation of his position. What were her family connections, what was their history? Oliver doubted anyone from the Ambrose line had taken a wife not of their society. He couldn't take her to be his marchioness, but it went against every grain and governing principle to take another woman to be his wife while Lily had such a hold over him.

How in God's name could he continue looking for a wife when the woman he had been searching for was now curled against his side, sleeping? Long red hair lay against the creamy flesh of her breast. Her lips were parted, her breath a soft flutter over his chest, and with a sigh, his name whispered from her lips. Oliver's heart tripped, and in that moment, he doubted he would ever be able to let her go. "Lily?"

"Hmm?"

"Come with me to London."

Her eyes cleared of the last fog of sleep, and she stared at him alertly. "You're going to town?"

"Yes. I'd meant to depart tomorrow. I've a few invitations from friends that I am compelled to honor."

"Why do you want me to come?"

"I want you to select a townhouse and a shop."

She sat up slowly, a frown marring her lovely face. "I don't understand."

He didn't, either. Oliver had sworn he wouldn't take a mistress and a wife at the same time. *Ah, bloody hell.* He would have to delay his plans to find a wife for the near future. Everything in him only clamored to be with her.

"You've agreed to be my mistress, yes?"

Her lips quivered, and then the lower one caught between her teeth. "Yes."

"Then I will set you up in a house in town, with servants and a carriage and an allowance. We'll visit Tattersall, and you can select a mare if you are of a mind to ride in Hyde Park. I know your shop is very important to you, so select one in High Holborn, and I will pay the lease for a year."

She bestowed on him a small, quizzical smile. "You don't need to do all of that. Your wealth and station aren't the reason I want to be your lover."

"I know." He gripped her hips and dragged her up the length of his body so that her lips hovered close to his. "Let me take care of you, Lily."

"I believe I can manage that on my own, and might I remind you that you still owe me a thousand pounds?"

Oliver smiled at her disgruntled tone. "I was simply hoping you would allow me the privilege of being a part of it."

"Do you think perhaps society will know I'm your mistress? I would not want any rumors to reach my parents, even though they are so buried in the country."

"We'll be discreet," he murmured.

Her eyes searched his intently, and he wondered if he was mistaken at the shadow of hurt lurking in her eyes.

"Lily, I—"

She stole the words from his lips in a soft but passionate kiss. He cradled her cheeks and ravished her mouth, groaning at her sweet taste.

They pulled apart, and she smiled. "Yes."

Fierce triumph clutched at his heart. "I will make the arrangements through my solicitor. Until then, you will stay with me in Grosvenor Square."

"Even so far removed in the country, my lord, I know that to be scandalous and quite improper."

"You are a widow and my mother's companion. I do not mean to be callous, my sweet, but we do not socialize with the same society for anyone to question your presence within my home. And it will only be until the lease on your townhouse is secured."

Her golden stare pierced him with unfathomable emotions. "I understand," she said softly.

"I'll also set you up with an allowance of—"

Her lips against his once again derailed his train of thoughts.

"You are already being overly generous, my lord. An

allowance is not necessary. You are helping me to secure a dream in a few weeks that might possibly take me years to accomplish. I thank you."

"It is my pleasure to take care of you."

"And it is my wish to not be fully dependent on your kindness. The profits from my shop will provide a more than sufficient living for my family and me."

"Then allow me to front you the money you will need for materials. Another thousand pounds added to what I owe you."

Her eyes widened at the sum. "My lord, in truth you do not owe me, for I did nothing to warrant the first promised thousand! I've not even sat for you as yet! This is remarkably silly."

As of their own accord, her fingers traced his lips. "I confess, you make me feel that silly. It's the only explanation, my sweet."

Excitement burned in her eyes and joy filled him at the myriad of expression chasing her features. She worried her bottom lips with her teeth for several seconds. "I can only accept on the condition that it is an investment, and you will be an investor in my business, with a twenty percent share."

There was something wonderful about her, something entirely unexpected. "Done."

"Oh, Oliver," she breathed and flung herself into his arms. An *oomph* escaped him as he tumbled back with her soft weight resting delightfully on him. Lily scattered kisses on his chin and lips, giggling her happiness. "I am dizzy with excitement at the possibilities!"

She rolled from his clasp and tugged on his banyan, which dwarfed her voluptuous figure. A sudden, inexplicable longing filled him to lay the world at her feet so that he could always bask in the radiance with which she currently glowed.

"I must retrieve my sketches and magazines. Oh,

magazines! Now I'll be able to subscribe to all the latest fashion magazines, even the one from Paris. I'll be right back, Oliver."

She faltered as she gripped the doorknob.

He frowned at the tension that sifted through her.

His lover pivoted on her heel to face him. "You are the Marquess of Ambrose. I am fully aware of what your duty to your title means. I'll not remain your mistress once you're married," she said with a proud tilt of her chin.

"I would not dishonor my wife so." Sentiments he had echoed for years now felt hollow to him. Lily Layton was a woman he wanted to know. He wanted to discover every hidden depth behind those lively intelligent eyes. His instincts warned him uncovering all of her would likely take him a lifetime. Eventually, he would select a bride.

Denial roiled within him. The very notion of giving up Lily left a bitter taste in his mouth. He would simply have to persevere when the time came. Except, Oliver wasn't sure he'd prove up to the task.

• • •

London was overcast, the atmosphere dreary and uninspiring. The streets were noisy, the bricked buildings grimy, and the scent wafting across the Thames was decidedly unpleasant. Lily smiled, for she wouldn't trade being in London at this very moment for anything in the world. The marquess's carriage rumbled over the cobbled road, taking her to High Holborn, where she was to meet with Oliver and his solicitor.

They had been in town now for three days, and she had been shocked at the efficiency with which he got things done. And how seamlessly things were achieved when one had money to spend without reservation. Lily had spent the day with several cloth merchants and had made a sizeable dent in her savings to purchase several bolts of muslin, calico, silk, and lace. She would start by making several elegant dresses for herself with her own unique flare. To secure the patronage she was hoping for, dressing modestly and unfashionably was not the way to see it done. She had some of the latest patterns from Paris and Venice, and ideas were already swirling in her head about some designs. She was eager to start sketching and cutting tonight. A smile tugged at her lips. But not before, of course, indulging in passion with her lover.

After dining together for the last few nights, he would sweep her into his arms, ravishing her with an intense passion that was sometimes frightening. They would talk for an hour or more before Oliver slipped away from her to attend some ball or stop in at his club. He would return before daybreak and make love with her again before succumbing to sleep. It was a pattern she found delightful, and one she could get used to. Except by next week, she should be in a house with her own servants and carriage. Lily could never have imagined that she, a simple country maid, would become the lover of a powerful lord. At times, when she lay atop him, replete and exhausted, a strange sensation would grip her. She fancied she saw a similar startled recognition in his gaze.

The carriage rolled to a halt, and a footman lowered the steps and assisted her down. She looked around at the lines of shops flanking each side of the road, anticipation blasting through her heart. The door to a shop on the left opened, and Oliver strolled out, appearing too wonderful in his blue superfine jacket, light brown breeches, and a top hat.

She went to him and clung to the arm he held out to her as they entered the shop. It was glorious. Far larger than she had anticipated, with several rooms. There was a sitting area at the front and another fitting area toward the back. There was a storeroom, and a workroom above with several shelves and cabinets where she would be able to store her work materials.

Lily was lost in her thoughts as she went through the rooms, mentally arranging everything to suit her purpose. This was more than she had ever dreamed of.

A lump grew in her throat, and she turned to him. "Thank you, my lord, I do not know how I will ever be able to repay your kindness."

He looked over at her, lifting a brow. "With twenty percent."

Lily grinned, then stepped to him and kissed his lips.

The solicitor flushed and quickly diverted his gaze.

"I've arranged for workers to be at your command for the rest of the week to organize and decorate the rooms however you want. I've also set up several accounts with merchants in town and drafted a bank note for two thousand pounds." Oliver turned to the solicitor with his arms around Lily's waist.

"Mr. Hodges."

The man's spine snapped straight. "Yes, my lord?"

"Whatever Mrs. Layton desires, see it done. You have my full approval to exceed that sum if the lady wishes."

Mr. Hodges bowed, his curious gaze flicking to her discreetly, then back to the marquess. "Yes, my lord."

Oliver faced Lily. "We've been invited to a dinner party tonight at the Duke and Duchess of Basil's home in Grosvenor Square."

Lily felt faint. "We?"

"Yes, my sweet. The duke, Radbourne, and I are very close friends. I do not know a finer man."

Somehow that assurance did little to assuage Lily's apprehension. "And they know…they know I am your lover?"

If he sensed any of her discomfort, he gave no indication. "Yes."

He clearly saw no issue with her meeting dukes and duchesses. *Good heavens.* Her sister would not believe Lily's tale. She smiled despite her anxiety. "And they want to meet me? A woman without any respectable connections?"

Oliver tucked behind her ear an errant lock of her hair that had escaped the confine of her bonnet. "You are a wonderful woman, Lily Layton. My friends want to meet the woman who seems to have captivated my senses, and I am sure they will like you."

The shop door closed, and she was startled to realize Mr. Hodges had slipped away. Lily shifted closer to Oliver, wrapping her arms around his waist and hugging him tightly.

"Are you well?" he demanded gruffly, resting his chin atop her bonnet.

"I am happy to be here with you, but there are times I am not entirely certain I am not dreaming. I am a simple country girl, with sometimes big notions, but none lofty enough to dine with dukes and duchesses."

"There will be earls and countesses as well."

"Oliver!"

"Just be yourself, Lily, and all will be well. I promise if you feel any discomfort, I will whisk you away immediately."

"Thank you," she said softly, breathing in his wonderful male scent and trying to feel confident about attending the dinner party. One that would possibly bring regret to his heart at having her at his side, for surely now he would see how wholly unsuited she was for his world and end their affair before it had truly begun.

Chapter Fourteen

A laugh pulsed from Lily's throat, and she tipped back her head, the graceful length of her throat on delightful display. There was no shame in her eyes or demeanor to know that it was evident to all she was his *chèr ami*.

His Lily glowed, and Oliver had never seen a more beautiful lady. Radbourne had been pleasantly shocked when he recognized her, but he had wisely refrained from commenting. Everyone had been so welcoming that Lily had relaxed, and the dinner party had been filled with lively conversation spanning Prinny's obsession with war, the struggles of soldiers, the arts, and the opera, and his love had kept pace effortlessly.

Nor did he detect a superiority of manner when his friends conversed with her. Quite the opposite, and ardent admiration was expressed by the duchess over Lily's dinner gown, which was apparently one of a kind. She wore a stunning ice blue gown of her own creation, with sleek and elegant lines and delicate lace trimmings. Oliver had gifted her with a brilliant sapphire necklace and earrings, which she wore, and Lily had caught her hair in an elegant chignon, with a few red tendrils teasing her cheeks. She looked soft and ravishing, and she was his.

The dinner ended, and the men were to retire to the library for port, and the ladies to the drawing-room. Instead, Oliver excused Lily and himself with a promise to return shortly. They strolled down the hallway, his lover laughing in delight.

"Oh, Oliver, your friends are wonderful. I never imagined it would have been so...so...splendid."

"You expected monsters, did you?"

The corners of her mouth lifted slightly, and he wanted to kiss that small smile. "More like rogues and scoundrels, and very proper, priggish countesses."

"My heart is relieved your expectations were exceeded."

They came upon a door, and he opened it, allowing her to precede him inside. A hearty fire burned in the grate, and several candles were lit, washing the large drawing room with a warm, inviting glow.

"Do you trust me?"

"Oh yes," she murmured, giving a sweetly sensual smile.

He reached into the inside pocket of his jacket and withdrew a slim leather book and handed it to her.

"My diary!"

"I've marked a page, will you read it?"

She shot him a quizzical smile but removed the bookmark. "Dearest Diary, I like watching others be intimate. Several nights I've touched myself to the memory of Lord R licking along Lady W's wet quim." She stopped, cleared her throat, then continued. "There is a dark need in me for men...and even women to see me naked. Would they admire my plumb curves, would they think I am beautiful, would they crave to taste my snatch, would they hunger to take me?"

His lover closed her diary, clearly unable to continue

reading her wanton thoughts.

"Have you read all of it?" she asked huskily.

"Several times. And I want to give you every desire written here," he murmured tapping the book. "I want to wipe away the shame I feel sometimes in your words. You are beautiful, Lily, inside and out. A woman of carnal heart, and that is never something to ashamed of. I quite admire you, and I want to please you in all ways."

She flushed a delightful pink. Oliver took the diary and rested it on the chaise. He tugged her to him gently and unpinned her glorious mane of hair, spreading it across her shoulders and décolletage. Lily's eyes darkened with anticipation, but when she lifted her beguiling mouth to his, instead of kissing her as her entreaty demanded, he dropped to knees.

She quivered. "You did not lock the door."

"That was deliberate."

A question flashed in her eyes, and she glanced back as the door opened and the Duke of Basil strolled in with his wife.

Lily jerked and then froze. The duke did not speak as he lowered himself into one of the six chairs artfully arranged in a semi-circle and drew his duchess onto his lap. Their avid stares did not move from Lily and Oliver in the center of the room. The door pushed open once more, and Lord Radbourne and Lady Wimbledon entered and commanded their respective seats.

His Lily trembled and glanced down at him. A thousand questions lurked in the beautiful depth of her eyes, along with a powerful flare of lust...and perhaps apprehension.

Lord R and Lady W, she mouthed.

I know, he, too, mouthed.

This time when the door opened, in sauntered Viscount Fenton and his wife, and Mr. Andrew Darby and his lover.

They, too, took their places, centering their undivided attention on his flower. Without breaking from Lily's gaze, he encircled her ankle lightly and pushed up, dragging her dress up and baring her stocking clad legs to their audience. Her breath hitched, and her eyes grew slumberous. Oliver leaned in and pressed a reassuring kiss to her stomach when she trembled. Using the gentlest of ministrations, soothing kisses along her inner thigh, he slowly undressed his lover, removing her stays, and dress, leaving her only in her pure white stockings and garters, and her delicately heeled silver dancing shoes.

Oliver stood and removed every article of clothing, dropping them beside hers on the floor. Lily's entire body was flushed pink, and her bottom lip quivered ever so slightly, but her expression was a study in sensuality. Gripping her hips firmly, he brought her to him, her breast flush with his chest, and took her lips in a deep kiss.

A soft, hungry sound purred from her before her lips parted, allowing him to dip into heaven. Her beautiful mouth and wicked tongue were the sweetest instruments of carnal torture. His muscles clenched with the force it required to hold back from dragging her up, wrapping her legs around his hips and rocking his cock into her deeply.

Somehow, she became the seducer, wresting control of their kiss, angling her mouth beneath his, tipping on her toes and taking his lips in a harder kiss. Oliver moaned as her mouth retreated then came back with light kisses, sensuous stings on his lower lips, then another deep, lascivious tangling of tongues.

Her lips trailed over his throat, over his chest and down. Sweet Mercy. This was not going entirely how he had planned their coming together here. He shouted as her tongue glided over his heavy and engorged cock.

"Lily," Oliver groaned, a thrust of his hips pushing him

too deep, but she took him, with such beguiling sensuality, he found himself gathering the silky curtain of her hair in his fist and slowly fucking her mouth.

She hummed her delight in pleasing him, the power she wielded over him and her captivated audience unchallenged. It was the most arousing thing he had ever seen, her lips stretching over his cock, her tongue flicking and curling over its engorged head as she knelt before him.

He blew out roughly, hanging on to his fragile control by his fingernails. She released him from the wet, tight grip of her mouth, leaned in and nipped the inside of his thigh, then soothed the sting with her tongue.

She stood, quite gracefully and surveyed their audience. Everyone seemed to be on edge, lust glowing from their eyes, their tenuous restraint hinted by the manner in which they gripped the armrests of their chairs. They wanted to touch… but could not. Lily knew it, the knowledge fueling the carnal power she held over them.

She tossed that glorious mane of dark red hair, which rippled over her shoulders and breasts like fire. She was a creature of sensuality as she tipped her head back and cupped her breasts, pinching her nipples.

The duke groaned, and Lord Radbourne surged from his chair to fist his hands at his side.

Possessive hunger roared inside of Oliver, and he went up behind her, clasped her hips, and kicked her legs wide to cup her mound quite possessively. He ran his fingers through her soft curls and down to part the lips of her tight cunt so they could see her pink, glistening flesh. Her breathing hitched, and she shuddered.

"She is mine," he growled. "Only mine."

The temptress in his arms moaned her approval. "As you are mine," she whispered achingly.

And he almost dropped to his knees at the promise of

love he saw in her eyes. Lily was one of the sweetest, kindest women he'd ever had the fortune to meet, to kiss, to hold, to converse with, to burn in lust and adventure. An undeniable knowledge filled his heart. He would never find another woman who would fit him this perfectly. His Lily radiated with warmth, lust, and such bravery and trust she humbled him. She deserved the world at her feet, and certainly more than just to be his mistress. A woman like her should not be hidden away or be made to feel less than any other. Her last husband had done that, and Oliver would be damned if he would continue his foolhardy ways. It would be a disservice to keep a woman as lovely and vibrant as Lily as a soiled dove, when she deserved the full richness of a family and acceptance.

He dipped his head and pressed a soft kiss to her temple. "You'll never regret being mine," Oliver vowed softly.

He walked her to the chair in the center of the room. "Kneel on it, my sweet."

She climbed atop the chair, her hands braced on the padded armrest, her ass arched delightfully in the air. He went behind her and gently pushed her knees apart until the very wet folds of her quim were bared to their audience.

She turned her head and looked back at them, her eyes daring them to touch, yet also challenging them to only watch. She was a pagan goddess. Oliver stepped back and stared, awed by her sweet wildness. He allowed his cock to nudge against the wet opening of her pussy and thrust to the heart of her in one smooth glide. She was that wet, and despite her slickness, her sheath hugged him in a fierce grip.

Her moan resonated with longing, pleasure, and arousal. *Take me*, she mouthed.

He felt his soul chaining to her as he fucked her, possessed her, loved her. And the awareness felt right. He loved Lily Layton. She was witty, kind, possessed a wonderful sense of humor, and stunning sensuality. For long moments there was nothing but the feel of his cock penetrating her slick channel. The sounds of wet sex and gasping cries wrapped around him until he could hear her sobbing for relief. He pressed his thumb on her pearl and rubbed.

She orgasmed in an exquisite burst, keening his name.

The stark pleasure of her pussy clamping and squeezing his cock ripped his climax from him, and with a hoarse shout, Oliver emptied his seed inside her. He hugged her to him, ignoring the moans from their audience that indicated they had succumbed to the carnality in the air.

Oliver pressed a kiss to her damp neck.

He loved this woman, and he needed to do something about it. Lily Layton would be his marchioness if she would have him. His mother was going to be scandalized, society would be appalled, but he would be happy if she would consent to be his wife. He hadn't forgotten her vow to never remarry.

Dear God, love me, Lily…

Chapter Fifteen

Three weeks after being in London, a few truths made
themselves evident to Lily. Despite her modest background
and connections, she had somehow become scandalous. Her
newfound notoriety had seen a drastic increase in her business,
so much so she had hired two additional seamstresses. It was
not only to the patronage of the Duchess of Basil and Lady
Wimbledon, or to Oliver's sound financial advice, that Lily
attributed her success. She also credited the tidbit that had
featured her in a scandal sheet.

> *Lord A, who is believed to be seeking a bride, has*
> *been seen recently with the fashionable Madam L*
> *taking a turn in Hyde Park, and at the Theatre Royal,*
> *Covent Garden. Society wonders at their connection.*

"If I should believe you, Lily, the very morning after this was
printed, you got fifty new patrons?" Her sister demanded with
incredulity, dropping the newspaper atop the stone counter
in the kitchen of their parents' cottage.

Her sister was her dearest friend, and Lily hid nothing

from her, so Mary Rose was quite aware of Lily's relationship with the marquess.

"Yes," Lily replied laughing. "London thrives on gossip."

"I cannot credit all you are saying," Mary Rose said with a gasping laugh. "*You*, declared as fashionable. Mamma and Papa will question where you got money from if you start giving it away." Mary Rose folded the bank draft of five hundred pounds Lily had given her and stuffed it into her apron pocket. "David won't know what to do with this fortune you're gifting us."

"He will be able to use some for his clinic and apothecary," Lily said. "And the children could get new boots and winter coats this year. And should you wish it, you can rent your own cottage."

Her sister's eyes glistened with tears.

"What is it, Mary?" Lily asked, putting down the potato she had been peeling.

"I'm with child again."

Equal pain and joy burst inside Lily. She wiped her hand on her apron and hurried to her sister and enfolded her in a warm hug. "I am very happy for you and David. Lizzie and Katie will be so happy."

"We are hoping for a boy," Mary said with a smile that wobbled. "Oh, Lily, how I wish you would find a similar happiness."

Lily stepped away and went back over to the stone counter to pick up the knife and potatoes. "Mamma is expecting this stew to be ready soon."

She could feel her sister's stare, but Lily couldn't bear looking at her, desperate to hide the pain that still lingered in her soul.

"David told me he informed you that it may still be possible," Mary said softly.

The knife clattered onto the table, and Lily gripped the

counter edges, steadying herself at the emotions that tore through her. "He did."

"Then why not remarry and—"

"I consulted with David when I failed to conceive with Robert after a year of marriage. Though David's words gave me some hope, it still did not happen."

"David said the frequency of how—"

"Mary Rose," Lily whispered. "I am not having this conversation with you!"

"Why not? I'm a married woman. I know full well what it takes to become with child," she snapped, blushing. "I am weary of avoiding the matter, and I hate that I feel so wretched that David and I have been blessed three times and you are alone."

Alone... An awful sensation took hold in Lily's stomach. When Oliver finally selected a wife, they would probably have children soon after. "I will never be alone," Lily said, facing her sister. "I have you and the children, and Mamma and Papa. I also have my shop. I am happy, Mary." Her assurances sounded hollow to her ears.

"Have you considered that you may get with child now that you and the marquess are lovers?"

She stared at her sister, unable to explain the pain that had driven her from London. Lily had woken four days ago in her lover's arms, her stomach cramping sharply, signaling her courses were near. "Lord Ambrose hardly leaves my bed, and I am still not with child," she finally answered, swallowing against the sudden tightness in her throat.

"My husband is the best doctor in Derbyshire. If he says there is a chance, there is," Mary said with a proud lift of her chin. "It took David and me four months after our wedding night before I got with child. How long have you been lovers with the marquess? A month? I daresay it is still possible, and you should turn your thoughts to what you would do if it happens. The resulting scandal would not be kind to you, or to our family, for a man of his station will not marry you."

Watching her sister as she moved about the kitchen, Lily felt an intense surge of love for her. Their mother entered the cottage, thankfully putting a stop to a conversation Lily would prefer to never have. She had indeed consulted with David a few years ago when her hunger for a child had left her restless many nights. He had even impressed upon her that less stress and more frequent coupling with the vicar would see the job done. He had even recommended a few vile tonics she had consumed to aid the process, and nothing had happened. Everything had felt hopeless then because frequent coupling was not something the vicar had wanted with his harlot wife. But since Oliver had entered her life, he had taken her every night, and in the days, too. Yet she was still empty. Not that she could be too disappointed. Lily couldn't imagine what she would do if somehow she ended up breeding. Her child would be a bastard.

Their mother withdrew the pie from the oven and set it on the cooling rack, then she checked on the stew.

"Vicar Smith and his lovely wife will be coming to dinner," she said, smiling. Light brown eyes, a perfect replica of her daughter's, twinkled. "I picked up a roast to add to the table." Mamma touched Lily's hand lightly. "I wore my new redingote, and it was so admired, my dear. I've been boasting about your shop in London. We're all so very proud of you."

Lily smiled, wondering what her mother would think if she knew it was the marquess that had made it possible.

I'm a mistress.

"Mamma! There is a carriage pulling in the driveway," Mary said, peeking through the small window of the kitchens. She paused in the kneading of the dough and glanced at their mother.

"A carriage? Oh, dear me," her mother fussed. "It

could be Squire Elkins and his daughter. I saw them at the butcher, and the squire hinted they might stop by for dinner. Everything has been so dreary for that family since his wife died." She pushed aside their curtain and peeked. "Upon my word, I do believe it to be the Marquess of Ambrose!"

The knife clattered from Lily's hand, the carrots she had been chopping forgotten. Why was Oliver there? She had left him at Belgrave Manor with the promise to return in a few days. Had something happened with the marchioness? Hurrying from around the worktable, she went to the water and basin and washed her hands.

"He's coming up to the door," Mary Rose gasped, her eyes rounding.

Their mother rushed from the kitchen. Lily untied her apron, balled it up, and dropped it on the counter before hurrying behind her mother into the small parlor where her father took his afternoon tea.

"What is it, my dears?"

"Lord Ambrose is coming to call," Mamma said, looking harried and excited in equal measure. Moving with quick efficiency, she fluffed the cushions on the sofa and put away her sewing basket and needles. "Mary, dear, put on the kettle and slice up the cake."

"The one for dinner?"

"Mary!"

Biting back her grin, Mary scampered away to do their mother's bidding.

A few moments later, a knock sounded. Squaring her shoulders, her mother left the parlor and then returned with Oliver. His eyes swept the small and tidy parlor before settling on Lily with such wonderful intensity. She blushed, certain her parents would correctly assess their tendre.

Papa bowed. "Lord Ambrose, it is an honor to have you in our home."

"Forgive me for calling so unexpectedly."

"Not at all," Mamma replied, turning on her heel to face the marquess. Lily knew the entire neighborhood would talk about this visit for weeks and her mother's importance would soar.

Lily stepped forward and faltered. How had she not noticed his jacket was grass stained and there was a tear in his trousers? "My lord! What happened? You are a mess."

"I raced with Radbourne along the lanes, and a dog appeared in the path. It is all murky, but I crashed my curricle."

"Good heavens, are you well?"

He gave the barest ghost of a smile, his gaze alarmingly intent upon her. "More so than I have ever been. For you see, I realize what a damn fool I'd been," Oliver said softy, his expression tender, and far too intimate with their watchful audience.

"A fool, my lord?"

He stepped closer. "A damn fool, Lily."

She endured a strange ache in her heart, and how Lily wished to rush to him and confirm that he was indeed well.

Mary Rose entered carrying a tray with cake and tea and placed it on their small walnut table. Oliver shifted and dipped his head in acknowledgment of her sister, and it was then Lily saw the blood at his temple.

"You're bleeding," Lily said, hurrying over to him, uncaring of her family's avidly curious and fascinated stares.

"It's nothing," he said smiling.

She glared at the blood pooling along his neckline. Clearly the accident addled his senses. "You have gone daft. We must return you home at once and summon the doctor. Or may I send for my brother-in-law, Dr. David Evans? He is our village doctor, and he is quite knowledgeable and proficient."

He placed a finger under her chin and lifted her gaze to

his. His touch, so light it was barely a breath of sensation, seemed to pierce her like an arrow. Her breath caught at the mix of emotions chasing his handsome features—hope, a hint of fear, and something that looked frightfully like love.

"Lily?"

A fine tremble went through her body. "Yes?"

He pushed a loose tendril behind her ear, his actions slow and tender. "Marry me, Lily Layton."

Her mother gasped and slapped a hand over her mouth, Mary Rose gaped quite unbecomingly, while her father slowly lowered himself to a chair, shaking his head.

Shock held Lily for long seconds, stealing her breath. She stared at Oliver for precious, heart-wrenching moments. "Upon my word, did you hit your head?"

He laughed, and she had never heard him sound so carefree and happy. "I did, but I assure you my wits are intact."

"I…" *Lord above.* He seemed sincere and eager…and in love. With her. A lump formed in her throat, and she wanted to shout with happiness but couldn't. "I cannot, my lord," she said stiffly, refusing to unravel and burst into raw, ugly tears.

"Lily?" her mother questioned, her eyes glowing with worry and disbelief.

He stepped back slightly. "Lily, I—"

"Please, Oliver, I have *nothing* to recommend me to the honor of being your marchioness. I'm the daughter of a country botanist. My first husband was a simple soldier and my second, the vicar of this parish, a friend of my father. I have no connections to offer you," she said hoarsely. "I have no money beyond the seventy pounds I've saved thus far. My reputation…" She cast her parents a quick glance, a blush heating her face. "We spend so much time together, Society possibly suspects I'm your mistress. I think…I believe that's all I can be," she whispered, wincing at the shock that bloomed on her mother and father's face.

"If you would grant us some privacy, I would greatly appreciate it," Oliver said to the room at large, seemingly unruffled by her rejection.

Her parents and sister discreetly left, closing the parlor door.

Lily's throat felt tight, and tears swam in her vision. He reached for her, and she lurched back, her leg hitting the walnut table, spilling the teapot and cakes onto the floor. It shattered, the sound echoing through the parlor. "I cannot speak of this now."

Ignoring Oliver, she skirted around the broken pieces and hurried toward the door. She could not face him now, and she desperately needed to be alone. Her composure needed to be regained, and the tearing emotions splintering through her heart must be controlled before she made a fool of herself. She flung the door open and rushed outside, not slowing her pace until she reached the gardens her father tended to so lovingly. There, she took several bracing breaths, but they did little to center her emotions. She had known being his lover would eventually end.

How I wish it were not so sudden and unexpected.

"Lily?"

She closed her eyes at Oliver's concerned tone and took a deep breath. Snapping her eyes open again, she squared her shoulders, lifted her chin, and faced him.

His eyes skimmed over her face with piercing intensity. "Do you love me?"

"I cannot marry you!" But dear God, she wanted to so much…so much.

"Yes, you can."

She opened her arms wide. "I'm…I'm nobody. I am without connections or the bloodline to make you a proper wife."

"You are *everything*, Lily. Generous to a fault, sweet,

passionate, intelligent—a woman I could see myself spending the rest of my life with. You are selfless, and I ardently admire you. I ask you to marry me, Lily Layton. I do not care about society's expectations, and despite the knowledge of my position and status, I am falling helplessly in love with you, and I do not want to stop it. We are not of the same privileged society, but your character elevates you far above many of my peers. Even above my own. You need not fear that you will not hold your own amongst my friends, for they already love and accept you, and even if they did not, I would tell them to sod off."

She slapped a palm across her mouth, staring at him helplessly.

"Today I raced along the lanes with Lord Radbourne. I crashed." He felt the back of his head gingerly. "I got a solid hit here, and for a few moments, as my world swirled and blackness hovered, all I thought of was you, Lily. Nothing else, no one else. Just you, my love. I did not think of duty, or the difference in our wealth and status. I thought of your face, your smile, the warmth that burns through my soul to know you are happy. Allow me to stand by your side, and I promise to cherish your gift in this life and the next."

My love... "Oliver," she breathed, shaking her head, dazed and out of sorts.

"I ask you again, my sweet, do you love me?"

"I will not answer that. Why ever would you ask me such a question?" Tears burned beneath her eyelids, and she willed them not to fall. "You know I have no wish to remarry."

"If you tell me you do not love me, right this moment, I'll walk away and never trouble you again with my sentiments."

He moved even closer to her, and there was no doubt in his eyes, as if he already knew the answer to his questions.

"What I feel for you does not signify. You are a marquess, a peer of this realm, and I—" She widened her arms. "I'm just a seamstress with no connection or money. What little reputation I had I already gave up by being your mistress."

A beautiful smile curved his lips, and within two strides, he was standing before her. He cupped her cheeks and kissed her. "We care for each other. Do we need any more reasons to spend the rest of our lives together?"

"I…"

"Do I make you happy, my sweet?"

"Oh yes," she said, pressing her forehead against his chest. The words David had said to her so many years ago ghosted through her thoughts. What if her brother-in-law was correct in his assessment? What if…what if she could have this wonderful man and a happiness that had seemed so impossible, she had not even dreamed it? Hope bloomed in her heart so fiercely it hurt. "I cannot give up my shop."

He rubbed soothing circles along her arm. "I didn't ask you to, nor would I require it."

"How unseemly it will be for me to own a business."

"You'll be my marchioness. Nothing will be impossible."

Damn her foolish, foolish heart and impossible hopes. "Yes, I'll marry you."

He crushed her to him in a fierce hug, and she returned his embrace, the happiness bursting in her heart none like she had ever endured.

Dear God, please let this be real.

Almost an hour later, Lily froze in the motion of knocking on the larger drawing room of Belgrave Manor. She had not been content to wait in the smaller sitting room while her love informed his mother of their news. Only now, perhaps she should have listened to her marquess.

"Upon my word, Oliver, you jest in poor taste!"

Lady Ambrose's shocked incredulity could not be denied,

and Lily flinched in embarrassment.

"I do not, Mother," his deep voice rumbled.

"To take a commoner for your bride? Our ancestry is noble and our bloodline impeachable. Mrs. Layton has no connections, no dowry, and I cannot think you would recommend her to be your marchioness. I've seen the way she looks at you, but I never thought you would succumb to her wiles. Take her to be your mistress. If the rumors floating about in town are rooted in truth, you've already established her as your *chèr ami*. Let her keep that role."

It was not as if she'd had any expectation Lady Ambrose would give her nod of approval to Oliver's notion of marrying her, but to hear her objections still pierced Lily deeply. Valiantly preventing her lower lip from trembling, she knocked once and then gently eased the door open. Oliver was sitting on his desk, his arms folded over his chest, his feet splayed casually. He seemed undaunted, and perhaps even slightly amused at his mother's complaints.

He glanced up, and the heat and love that flashed in his eyes stole her breath. Willing her gaze away from his, she turned to the marchioness, who observed her with a narrow-eyed glare. A flush swept up Lily's face, but she marshaled her emotion, lifted her chin, and sauntered farther into the drawing room.

"My lady, my lord," she greeted, dipping into an elegant curtsy.

Oliver rose with fluid grace and strolled over to Lily. He laced their fingers together, and she glanced down at their entwined clasp, a lump forming in her throat. Somehow, she had thought his convictions would have trembled at his mother's protest.

"Why are you marrying me, Lily?"

She snapped her gaze to his, and a shiver of delight went through her heart at the tender way he smiled at her. "Because I love you with a passion I've never felt for another,"

she whispered, her voice hoarse with too many emotions—
joy, apprehension, hope.

"I promise, Mother," Oliver said, without taking his
regard from Lily, "it is because I love Lily that I've asked her
to be my wife, my friend, my marchioness, and no other will
do. You will not make her uncomfortable in any respect. To
wound her is to wound me, to deride her is to hurt me, and if
you love me, you'll love her, for she is more, far more than the
social class she was born to."

I may not be able to give you an heir... The words trembled
on her lips, but Lily repressed the doubt and directed her
attention to the hope her brother-in-law had given her. There
was a rustle, and Lily shifted as the marchioness surged to her
feet. She braced herself for vitriol that never came. Instead,
Lady Ambrose smiled, her kind eyes crinkling at the corner.

"I never thought I would live to see you so happy, my
son." She walked over to them, her hands held forward. Lily
grasped one, and Oliver the other.

The marchioness leaned in and kissed Lily's cheek.
"Forgive my earlier utterances. I must say, I was shocked, but
now I see how you look at each other, and that is what I've
always wanted for my son. I already love you, Lily. Surely you
must know that. I must warn you, society will not be kind,
and there will be those who are offended by your union. I will
support you both because I love you."

Lily almost wept her relief. "Thank you, my lady."

"No, thank you, Lily. I'm quite pleased to see my son so
delighted."

Then, after kissing Oliver, the marchioness swept from
the room, leaving them alone and the door slightly ajar.

Lily smiled. "Do you suppose she does not realize how
improper and scandalous we've been?"

He tugged her close and pressed a kiss to her forehead.
The sweetest ache filled her heart. "Oliver?"

He pressed another impossibly soft kiss on her throat. "Hmm?"

"I feel as if I am in a dream."

"You're my heart, Lily. I promise you won't regret marrying me. All who don't approve of our union can go hang."

"I promise you won't regret marrying me, either. I'll read all the books on etiquette, and I'll be a very attentive student as you teach me all the dances." She gasped as he placed another kiss on her throat and tilted her head back, allowing him access to the curve of her jawline. "I'll not shame you," she vowed fiercely. "I'll be a wife you will be proud of."

Her marquess took her lips in a fiery kiss, and Lily giggled as he swept her into his arms and walked with her over to the door. Without releasing her lips, he managed to push it closed.

She pulled from him. "They'll know what we're doing!"

"They'll need to get used to doors in our homes closing for hours in the middle of the day."

She laughed.

He dropped his forehead to her with a sigh. "Are you desiring a large wedding?"

"This was never something I had to think about. What do you want?"

"You," came his swift and possessive reply.

What if this is naught but a dream?

"Something small and beautiful," she whispered. "With our families and close friends. And I'll be wearing the most glorious dress, inspired by a Parisian design, with layers of silk and the hem trimmed with lace and beads."

"Pearls and diamonds."

Lily laughed. "Oh, Oliver, this feels too wonderful to be true. I never thought I would ever be this happy."

And as her lover kissed her, Lily dearly prayed the hope that bubbled in her soul would flower and bear fruit.

Chapter Sixteen

"The Marquess and Marchioness of Ambrose!"

A hush fell over the elegantly decorated ballroom of the Duchess of Basil as Lily and Oliver appeared on the landing, their first public appearance after the news of their marriage had roared through the *ton* several weeks ago. She glanced at her husband, not liking the anxiety that scythed through her heart. The dratted man winked.

"They will love you," he murmured. "And remember, if they don't, they can..."

"Go hang," she finished with a wide grin.

"You are the most ravishing woman here."

Lily felt particularly beautiful in her emerald high cinched waist gown, with its short, ruffled sleeves and scandalous décolletage. Her dancing slippers were golden and matched the gold threads woven through her upswept hair.

"Flattery will always get you whatever you wish, my husband."

Their hosts and hostess, the Duke and Duchess of Basil, greeted Lily and Oliver. "You are a curiosity, my dear—the commoner who snagged one of the most eligible lords of the season," the duchess said, her eyes twinkling with pure devilry.

It seemed as if all of refined society had crammed into the duchess's grand ballroom and were staring. Lily never imagined his set was so ridiculous.

"My dear friend, how truly marvelous you look tonight," Elizabeth said, the duchess of Basil, looping her hands through Lily's. The duchess glanced at Oliver. "Allow me to introduce your darling to a few ladies who have been quite eager to make her acquaintance. Everyone has been clamoring to meet her after the scandal of your marriage and departure to Venice."

Lily nodded, amused despite the collective throng following her and the duchess's progress through the room. Lily glanced back at Oliver and winked, letting him know she was quite unintimidated by society's rabid curiosity. She hadn't idled the weeks away while they had been abroad. She had read many books on the proper decorum a lady should possess.

They had shocked society when they had wed within a week of Oliver asking Lily. The scandal that had roared through the *ton* had been blistering, if the numerous newspaper articles were anything to judge by, but they had weathered it by traveling from Dover to Calais on her marquess's private yacht. They had visited Paris, mostly to shop, and then traveled onward to Venice, uncaring of the rest of the world as they burned in mutual sensual delight. He'd shown her all the wonderful places that had inspired the artist in him, and she had posed for him many times. Now his private collection had erotic paintings of his marchioness the rest of the world would never see. Well, at least not while they were alive.

"My dear Minerva," Elizabeth said to Countess Brenton.

"May I present my dear friend, Lily, the Marchioness of Ambrose."

The countess dipped into an elegant curtsy, and Lily gracefully inclined her head. The many introductions blurred, and she felt like an insect under a microscope as they analyzed and dissected the commoner who had somehow beguiled their charming marquess.

"Lady Ambrose, rumors suggest you have a personal stake in a dressmaker's shop."

"How outrageous!"

"You were married twice before, I've been told?"

"Your ball gown is the most delightful I've seen this season."

"Upon my word, it is true what they say? It's a love match between you and the marquess?"

Varied conversations swirled around her, and the heat of the ball was almost stifling. Lily pulled away from the ladies as a waltz was announced. She turned on her heel, and suddenly her love was there, gathering her in his arms and leading her to the dance floor.

"I've got you," he murmured, pressing a fleeting kiss to her lips and ignoring several shocked gasps.

Lily laughed, delighted with his wickedness. He twirled her across the floor with his unique grace, and Lily had never felt happier. After the waltz ended, they scandalized the society present by dancing at least three more times together before Oliver whisked her away from the ball toward a darkened hallway.

"I've been burning to kiss you," he murmured.

She paused and lifted her mouth to his.

"Not on these lips," he said dragging his thumb across her mouth.

A blast of heat tore through Lily, thinking of where he wanted his mouth and how he would make her burn.

Her marquess stealthily opened a door and urged her inside a room where a fire burned low in the grate. Shadows danced from the low flame, but Lily recognized they were in the library.

She froze as a whimpering cry echoed in the room. Lily's breath strangled as she realized Elizabeth was seated atop her duke, riding him with wanton intensity.

Oliver pressed into her back as he closed the door gently, so as not to startle the duke and duchess.

"We shouldn't be here." She shivered even as a flash of arousal burned through her.

"I thought you would approve," he growled.

"You knew they'd be here," Lily whispered, entranced with the picture the duchess presented, seated on her duke's cock, her mass of dark hair rippling down her back, his large hand firmly gripping her buttocks as he slammed her down on his shaft, over and over.

A soft moan whispered past Lily's lips as the duke lifted his duchess off him, spun with her, and placed her on the desk and buried his face against her cunt.

The fire burned lower and lower, painting the lovers in soft, erotic light. The duke was well muscled, his form powerful and lean, and with a large and ruddy cock. As if they had a will of her own, Lily's feet moved soundlessly over the plush carpet as she crept closer. A dark, wanton heat speared her. She liked watching, and she enjoyed it all the more knowing the duke and duchess had no notion they had a voyeur.

He flipped his duchess around, then reached for something on his desk. A lavender scent rode the air. Oil. He pushed a cushion beneath her hips and splayed her wide.

Lily shifted so she could see around the duke's broad shoulders. He did not reach for his wife's wet quim, but the forbidden entrance below. He oiled her and his cock, then positioned himself and drove deep until he was buried to the hilt.

The duchess's wild cry was one filled with pain...and pleasure.

Laden heat surged through Lily as she watched her friend's ravishment. Was this how Elizabeth had felt when she had watched Oliver debauch her? This heat? This clawing lust to spread her own legs and beg her husband to fuck them to repletion?

"Do you want to join?" Oliver growled at her ears.

Lily sagged against him, grateful for the support of his strength. She never knew hunger could be this painful...this needy...and yet, she only wanted to be an observer.

"I just want to watch."

"Then watch," he murmured, kissing along her neck. "Look at how his cock is parting those tight muscles. He isn't treating her like a glass that can be broken, or a lady that should be coddled. His duchess is his wife, his queen, but she's also his mistress, his whore. He doesn't hold back when he's fucking her because he loves her and can be unrestrained with his duchess without judgment."

Lily swallowed. "Look at her face," she whispered. "Do you see the love, the lust, the knowledge that she's more than his duchess? She knows, Oliver...just like I know I am your everything. Your lover, your wife, your marchioness, your whore. What he's doing to her is wrong, depraved, maybe a sin, but she doesn't care, and I don't care. All that matters is the pleasure, the trust, and the love that blaze in her soul for her duke right now. I know because the same love and wanton submission burn in my heart for you."

With a scream of her husband's name, Elizabeth unraveled, and her duke gave a hoarse shout, then jerked in her arms and thrust several more times before stilling.

Then the duchess laughed, the sound soft, and loving.

The duke bent his head and kissed her lips, his actions so tender a lump formed in Lily's throat...and then he bent even farther and kissed her stomach.

"Your mother will be the death of me," he whispered.

Lily and Oliver both froze.

"We should leave now, "Lily whispered, as the duke and duchess hugged each other.

Oliver deftly opened the door and ushered Lily into the hallway. There, they paused and took a few breaths together.

"That will be us soon," Oliver said. "I cannot say what I desire more, a son or a daughter with your eyes and smile."

This was the first in the three months they had been married her marquess mentioned children. *Dear God.* Guilt and fear wrapped their terrible hands around her heart and squeezed. "I..."

Concern flashed in those beautiful dark blue eyes peering down at her. "My sweet, are you well? You've gone terribly pale."

"I need a breath of fresh air," she gasped, deftly slipping from Oliver's arms and hurrying down the hallway toward the terrace door. Lily spilled outside, heaving, her throat tightening.

She had seen her brother-in-law a few weeks ago in Hampshire when she had presented to him and Mary Rose the keys for a large and well situated five-bedroom cottage. Lily had once again mentioned her lack of conceiving. David had tried to reassure her it was still possible, but she had seen the pity in his eyes. Her husband made love to her over and over, in so many varied ways, and she remained a hollow husk. Lily hated that she was once again reducing herself to despair, when she had clawed from it once already and had been content to remain in the life she had carved for herself.

It had taken some time to admit it to herself, but she wanted a family, too, and not just for Oliver, but for herself.

She had buried the hope so deep inside, refusing to let it out...but now, she felt scraped raw with tearing emotions she had no notion how to accept.

Damn Oliver for making her feel again, damn him for making her hope for the impossible, damn him for being a marquess, and damn him for making her love him so desperately she could not imagine life without him. There was no doubt she would lose him once she revealed her condition. He would have the grounds for a divorce, and while the scandal of it would be terrible indeed, surely, he would prefer that to the end of his lineage.

"Lily, my sweet, what is it?"

Her love clasped her hand and spun her to face him.

She was perilously close to tears. She hugged his arms to her body. "Oh, Oliver...I...I am simply overwhelmed with Elizabeth's news. I do so hope very much for a similar joy for us. In fact, I feel quite desperate to secure an heir for you." She hadn't brought anything to their marriage, and she dearly wished she could at least give him what every lord needed. And she wanted it so very much, too.

Oliver smiled. "Don't be. I am too enraptured by what we have to want another in our life just yet. Perhaps I should even be taking precautions, for I want you to myself at least for another two years before we start making heirs and spares."

Tell him it may never happen... "I—"

He kissed her, over and over, stealing her fear and replacing it with love and arousal. And as she burrowed into his wonderful warmth, Lily once more suppressed the insidious doubt.

He whisked her deeper into the gardens, away from the revelry of the ball, his devilishly skillful fingers quickly arousing her to a fevered pitch. He rolled her nipples between his thumbs and forefingers, gentle, then hard. They tumbled to the grass, and with a grunt, he took the brunt of their fall.

Lily giggled, and he captured the sound with another deep kiss. He intoxicated her senses so.

Her husband ravished with devastating expertise, and she responded, unable to deny what he did to her body. Oliver made love to her in the dark and secluded gardens, compelling Lily to remember nothing but this burning need that existed in their hearts.

Chapter Seventeen

Six months later…

Oliver closed the business ledger, unable to concentrate on his investment reports. A cold knot of dread had been lingering in his heart this past week. His wife was unhappy. The shift in her temperament had first appeared five nights ago when, for the first time since their marriage, she had not slept in his arms. His wife had used the connecting door to their chambers to slip into her room. He had stirred awake as the door closed softly, and he had pushed from the bed, opened her door, and almost roared in denial as her soft sobs had reached his ear.

Had he been too rough? He had taken her mouth with his cock, then her ass, and he hadn't been gentle. She had hummed with pleasure and had been just as eager, but there had been an unfathomable emotion in her beautiful eyes that had given him pause several times.

Had he disgusted her when he had held her throat and massaged, urging her to take his thickness all the way to the back of her throat? Or had it been when he had closed her legs tightly together, placed them over his right shoulder, and slipped his oiled prick deep into that forbidden entrance? That had been the third time he had taken her like that, and Oliver admitted he had ridden her a little longer, a little harder, and had been extremely filthy with his praise.

He had slipped into the bed beside her and held her while she cried. Oliver had probed and demanded an answer, but Lily had provided none. They had been so open and wonderful with each other for the past several months that a terrible sensation had started to grow in his heart.

Was it that she no longer enjoyed the way in which he made love with her?

Oliver had then made a concentrated effort to make love to her, sweet and gentle, for the last few nights, suppressing all his carnal inclinations. Yet it did not work. She grew more distant, the brightness of her smile had dimmed, and last night, when he had pressed a kiss against the hollow concave of her stomach and dipped his tongue into her navel, she had been frozen like a block of ice. And once again she had slipped away to her chamber when she thought he slept.

He pushed from behind his desk and strode from his private study. He climbed the steps rapidly and made his way to his bedchamber. It was empty. Biting back the frustration, he spun on his heel. He would check the drawing rooms, and perhaps the gazebos outside. An awareness had him faltering, and he spun around to consider their connecting door. He prowled over to it, and faint sounds reached his ear. Without knocking, he opened the connection and hesitated at the threshold of his marchioness's chamber. She was sitting on the sill of the large window overlooking the graceful gardens of Belgrave Manor. There was an air of melancholy about her he did not like.

No more. He would not have a marriage that was cold and filled with doubt and fear. He was not his damned father, and if his marchioness was disgusted by his constant depraved demands, he would do everything in his power to curb his dark needs. She had always been genteel, and he had corrupted and debauched her purity with his unceasing lust. His Lily was worth anything, even giving up the desires he thought he couldn't do without. Nor would he take a mistress if she wanted a gentler brand of loving, and it was time he proved it to her.

. . .

The joy had slowly been dimming in Lily's heart, and as she rubbed the ache in her stomach, which heralded the arrival of her monthly courses, the last vestige died. She had been the Marchioness of Ambrose for nine months, and her husband made love to her with unwavering passion almost every night. She adored him with a breadth and intensity she had not thought possible, and she had failed him. The loss of something that she hoped so much for was unbearable. How silly it had been for her to believe not one, but two husbands had been the failure and not her. And her foolish hope had allowed her to commit a most unforgivable and grievous sin. How would she inform Oliver?

The fear and doubt that knotted through her was crippling, and she wanted to sink to her knees on the plush carpet. Instead, she remained frozen where she sat, overlooking the beauty of their estate. A light snow blanketed the landscape, the blood red roses a shocking contrast to the white purity. Lily hugged herself and struggled for strength. How long could she continue to keep her silence? The more time she allowed to pass, the more Oliver would judge her.

Taking a deep breath, she stood and squared her shoulders. The realities must be faced, and she truly could no longer continue to keep him in the dark. But first, she would respond to the multitude of invitations awaiting her and read the report from madam Marie Delacroix, the head seamstress at Lily's shop on High Holborn. While she did not partake in the day to day running of the business, Lily sent her designs and creations to Marie, a wonderful artist who brought Lily's genius to life in the most incredible way. She had achieved her dream and had been featured several times in fashion magazines for the daring and unique styles she wore. Little did society know that she wore styles fashioned by her, and that was why she seemed to be the pioneer of the latest fashions.

She was also due to visit tenants with Oliver before they departed next week to London for the season. Lily turned and gasped, her hand fluttering to her chest. Her love entered her chamber and slowly closed the door.

"You startled me, my lord. I'd not heard you."

His expression was guarded as he sauntered toward her. "Is everything well, my love?"

Warmth tunneled through her, and she hurried to his arms. With a relieved groan, he enfolded her into a hug and pressed a kiss to the top of her hair. The tension leaked from her, and she inhaled his wonderful scent into her lungs.

"Lily, my darling, you've been out of sorts for a while now, and I can see your unhappiness."

She lifted her lips to his mutely, hating that tears spilled down her cheeks. How he would resent her once she admitted her sin. Why had she persuaded herself that it would be different? *Dear God, why?* The anger and disappointment he would feel that she could not do her duty to him would be horrible. If her marquess so desired, he had the wealth and power to divorce her and find another who would be more suitable to be his marchioness. But the resulting scandal would be terrible. More so than Oliver marrying his mistress, a woman of inferior rank. No doubt those who did not approve of their unlikely match would now celebrate.

He eased her from him, his thumb caressing the tear across her cheeks. "Have I been too rough with my passions?" he asked gruffly. "That night in the gazebo..."

Her heart lurched. "No! You were more forceful, but I loved every moment. When I am in your arms, it's the best place on earth. I thought the four times I climaxed was proof of that."

He lifted her chin with his finger, and his eyes searched her face in a thoroughly disturbing fashion. "Then why have you been pulling from me? Why do you creep from my embrace and come to this room to weep as if your heart is breaking?"

She hadn't realized he'd been aware she cried when she left their bed. "I...we've been married for nine months," she said softly, pulling away, hating that she was leaving the safe shelter of his arms.

"I would think that was cause for celebration and not the sorrow I can see in your gaze. Tell me, my love...I will slay all your dragons."

Unexpectedly, Lily burst into raw, ugly tears.

Alarm flared in Oliver's eyes, and he scooped her into his arms and sat in the chaise lounge by the fire, cradling her protectively against his chest. "Lily, my sweet, you are killing me."

"I deceived you in the most horrid manner, and you'll have no choice but to banish me from your life and heart."

He stiffened and then relaxed, hugging her even closer. "You are being dramatic. There is nothing in this world that can kill my love for you. Now, tell me, my sweet, why you are crying?" he asked gruffly.

A ragged breath tore from her. "Do you want children, a beloved son to groom as your heir, a daughter to cherish and spoil?

"Of course I desire children."

She squeezed her eyes closed tightly. Taking a deep breath, she pried them open and pushed from his lap. Clasping her hand together in front of her, she lifted her chin and tried to feel brave. Instead, she felt like a prisoner going to the executioner block. "I am barren."

He jerked as if she had punched him in the gut. "Lily, sweetheart, you cannot know that—"

"No," she whispered fiercely. "I do know, Oliver. I've been married twice and have produced no issue. The vicar wanted children, so the village doctor was summoned. He confirmed that...that I cannot fall with child."

A flash of pain, so deep it seared her soul, flared in his eyes before his expression shuttered.

Lily almost fell to her knees, wanting to scream her regret and fear. "I was never fit to be your marchioness. Perhaps your soiled dove, but nothing more, and I allowed my foolish heart and desperate hopes to convince me otherwise...and now...I've trapped you in a doomed marriage. How can I ask your forgiveness and expect it?" She thrust trembling fingers through her hair. "I cannot... I cannot grant you...us a family."

He remained remarkably still.

Lily had no notion of why she waited. There was nothing he could say, for she saw the truth in his eyes.

"I'll summon Dr. Bramwell and—"

"I've already seen a doctor. My brother-in-law. He is the most respected doctor in the village, and he is quite knowledgeable. He...he told me that it may never happen, given how long we've been married while I remain childless." She kept her face averted, unable to bear seeing the abject disappointment and betrayal in his eyes. "I knew before we married there was the strongest possibility of me not being able to produce an heir, but I truly thought it would be different this time."

Finally, he spoke. "Why didn't you tell me?"

She sobbed. "I was afraid, and I was hopeful that the problem wasn't me. In one week, you made love to me more than my two husbands combined. I had hoped...how I hoped that was the reason I never swelled with child. I thought, with how often we were wrapped in each other's arms, I would most certainly give you a child to love...an heir. I prayed the hollowness inside me would be filled."

She had expected him to shout his anger and frustration. Instead, his face was a mask of cold, studied indifference, which hurt far worse than his anticipated anger. She did not deserve the honesty of his reactions now, but dear God, she needed them. "Do not hate me," she said hoarsely. Which was an impossible request. "I...I've been reading, and I know it is your right to seek an annulment based on the circumstances."

She braved looking at him and flinched. He'd stood, and there was a bleakness in his eyes she had never seen before. "Oliver...I...I don't know what to do. I am not brave enough to walk over to you now and hug you, but that is what I want to do more than anything in this world."

Her husband remained silent, and in that moment, Lily knew he would never be able to forgive her. She saw the dreams in his heart for a family shatter.

"I made a mistake, I should not have married you. I'll leave... Oh God, I'll leave. I will pack my trunk and leave immediately," she cried.

Her husband was chillingly detached, and she wanted to howl from the pain tearing through her heart. "I'm so sorry," she whispered, then turned from the room and ran.

Lily ran away from her actions, the pain, the fear, and the cold condemnation in her husband's eyes.

Chapter Eighteen

Oliver stared at the open doorway his wife had just fled through. Good God, how had it all come to this? It had never once occurred to him that such a possibility existed. Even when his mother had complained a few times that she heard no news of his nursery being filled, he'd firmly told her to direct her energies to her own life, considering she had moved to the dowager cottage in Kent.

There was piercing pain in his heart that he hardly knew what to do with. He left the chambers and made his way downstairs and outside into the bracing cold. Inhaling deeply, he walked along the path that would take him to the lake. Taking a wife and then having children was simply an expectation he'd had from childhood—the necessity of his rank and his duty to his title. He had craved a family, but the idea of a wife, a woman to fulfill his needs had been a more tangible dream than imagining children. Over the last few months, though, he had thought of them, of the pride he would feel seeing Lily swollen, the joy of having a daughter as radiant and intelligent as her, of having a son who would possibly emulate his ways. The loss of a dream he had just allowed into his heart felt like a blunt stake being hammered through his chest. He touched the spot above his heart that ached like a physical wound.

And Lily had known there was the possibility of them never having a child, of them never fulfilling his duty.

He absorbed the pain filling his soul and was mildly shocked at the tears that smarted his eyes. How did his wife feel? She would have been aware of this loss for years. The pain she must have endured, and what she must feel now at revealing all to him, gutted Oliver.

Anguish rolled through him like poison coursing through his veins, and he wanted to release the brutal hold he had on his emotions and weep. For he understood that he had lost his Lily. She expected him to divorce her, and she would push him to it, for what lord did not hunger for a spare and an heir.

How could she even think for a moment he would let her go?

She would not allow him to comfort her, protect her, and share the pain. She would withdraw as she had been doing for the last week, cutting off her love and emotions from him. *Ah, fuck.*

A crunch against snow had him shifting to see who had intruded. Radbourne. He'd forgotten the earl and Lady Wimbledon had planned a visit. Oliver was going to be a discourteous ass, but now was not the time for guests.

The earl assessed him with a frown. "Good God, Ambrose, has someone died?"

The boulder pressing on his chest grew heavier. "No, but I fear now is not the time for a visit. Please extend my apologies to Lady Wimbledon ."

Concern flashed in his friend's eyes as he said, "We had a row. She did not come down with me."

Oliver turned back to the tranquil waters of the lake.

Radbourne stood beside him, a silent support Oliver did not desire. "Don't you have somewhere to be?"

Radbourne did not reply for several moments, then he said, "The last time I saw such a look in your eyes, you had just learned of your father's death."

Oliver stiffened. There was some truth to the earl's statement. He couldn't shake the feeling that his soul had been ripped from his body. He had no notion of how to make Lily see that they could survive whatever storm life threw their way. Hell, he had no notion how they would survive this hurdle, but losing her was not an option for him. Everything in him clamored to go to her, but what would he say? Her eyes had seemed so desolate. "My marchioness is barren."

"Christ." There was a silence, then the earl said, "Will you divorce her?"

Disbelief scythed through Oliver. "Do you truly believe such a thing possible of me?"

"You have a duty to your title," Radbourne rebutted softly. "No one would fault you if you sought an annulment on those grounds. Surely, she must have known. That, my friend, is fraud."

He faced his friend. "I believe my wife arrived at the same conclusion." How little faith she had in him and his love. "I do not feel betrayed that she did not tell me. What I feel is fear I will lose her."

Confusion marred his friend's expression. "Fear?"

"How do I convince the woman I love more than my title, more than duty and obligation, that she has not failed me? How do I comfort her when her arms will remain empty, her womb hollow, and the one thing she wants more than anything I am unable to grant her?"

"What will you do?" the earl asked gruffly.

"Haunt her as the mere idea of losing her haunts me. I cannot...will not let her go." Even if it meant battling her fears for all the time they would be together.

• • •

Lily stood with her hands pressed against the cool window pane. Her love stood by the lake, and she so desperately wanted to go to him. But what could she say? What could she do? She didn't have to imagine the pain and disappointment he felt—she knew it too keenly. Letting him go was the hardest thing she would ever face in her life. She wanted to scream and rail, but he was a peer of the realm and needed an heir. It was also more than that. Oliver was so giving and wonderful, a man like him should have several children to shower with affection.

It took all of Lily's fortitude to turn from the window and walk over to the bell pull and ring for her maid.

A few minutes later the door opened. "You rang, your ladyship?" Millie said with a smile.

"Yes." Lily cleared her throat. "My trunks need to be packed and the carriage ordered to be ready."

Millie's eyes widened at the unexpected request. "Yes, my lady," she said, dipping into a curtsy and rushing from the chamber.

Lily swallowed and walked stiffly over to the armoire. She opened the door and started to take down her gowns, her mind churning. Where would she go? Not to their townhouse in London or their manor by the seaside in Dover. It would be best if she returned to her parents' cottage, or perhaps she would stay with Mary Rose for a bit. When the *ton* got a whiff of their separation, the scandal would be horrible. Her throat went tight, although she truly did not care about the gossip to come. She had lost the man she had fallen so irrevocably in love with.

She lingered over a dark red wine gown, caressing the

taffeta between her thumb and forefinger. Lily recalled the night she had worn this gown, a few weeks past in London. They had strolled through the lantern-lit walks of Vauxhall Gardens, chatting together. Lily had felt so happy and free and cherished as their enchanted evening had captivated her senses. Her marquess had wickedly seduced her, out in the open where anyone could have come upon them. She lifted the dress to her face and inhaled deeply, thinking she could still smell their passion, hear his masculine chuckle of satiation afterward, feel the gentle kiss he had pressed across her brow.

Anguish tightened her throat. A raw, ugly sound was wrenched from the depth of her being, and the tears came freely. *I can't do it. Dear God, I can't leave.*

Pressing her hand against her stomach, she inhaled deeply, trying her best to control the pain and doubt tearing through her heart. She would go to him, but what would she say?

A whisper of sound had her spinning around. Oliver stood in the doorway, his cold blue eyes scanning the gowns dumped on the bed in such disarray. He could possibly banish her from his sight forever, but the knowledge he was trapped without a future for his title would haunt him terribly. It would be an annulment, then. She masked the tumult of her emotions and steeled her spine, waiting for words that she feared would forever wound her most deeply.

"Have you forgotten our vows so easily?"

Her lips parted, then quivered slightly. "No, of course not," Lily said hoarsely.

He scrubbed a hand over his face and sighed; the defeat in the sound dragged a flinch from her. "Have I been such a poor husband, have I been so shallow in character, you believe I would cast you aside?"

She recoiled at the bleak pain and anger that flashed deep

in his eyes. "You have been...you are wonderful, my lord."

Oliver watched her like a hawk. "You can leave. I'll not stop you."

Lily almost crumpled to the carpeted floor at that declaration.

Then he took one step closer. "But wherever you go, so shall I."

Her eyes widened, and she stared at him, confusion rushing through her. "I do not understand."

"Did you not swear before God that you would love me, always?"

"Yes," she whispered, fearing the hope that twisted through her heart. Her heart was beating too fast. Lily dropped the gown onto the carpeted floor, skirted around the pile of silk, and took a few steps toward him. She halted in the center of the room. "You will resent me," she said hoarsely.

"Wrong," he ground out with such force she gasped. "I do not love you because I hoped you would give me children, nor does that define the woman you are. I fell in love with your generosity of spirit, your unmatched sweetness and vigor for life, and your wonderful sensuality. I would be pleased if we were so blessed, and I dare say I would be happy. But not happier than I am with you in my life and my heart. I do not feel the pain as keenly as you do, my sweet, but I implore you to give me the chance to grieve with you, to hold you close when it gets unbearable. I want to be with you when you are happy, and I shall certainly be there when you're despondent."

Oliver walked over to her and cupped her cheek, an echo of something dark and painful lingering in his eyes. "My greatest fear now is that I will never be able to make you happy because I cannot give you your heart's desire. To see your pain and to hear your sobs is like acid against my skin."

Her lower lip trembled with the effort to prevent the tears

from spilling. "That is how I feel to know I cannot give you a child."

"My heart's desire is you, Lily...only *you*."

There was something in his soft declaration, about the way he waited for her, his patience, that shattered the cold knot of doubt inside her. "I love you, too, so desperately, but—"

"There is no but." His mien was implacable, and the awareness that this man would not let her go weakened her knees.

"We'll never have a child."

"I know."

She shook her head, dazed at the intensity of the emotions twisting through her. "There will be no heir."

"I have a cousin, and he has sons for when the need arises."

"There'll be no sons or daughters, no sweet and unfettered laughter echoing along these hallways for us."

"I know." Then there was a thick, heavy silence that echoed with so many questions...and with hope.

"And I still want you forever, Lily." He kissed her, a mere brush of his lips over her, softly brushing away her tears with his thumb. "I am nothing without you in my life, my sweet."

The tight, wonderful ache in her chest threatened to consume her. "Oliver..." she murmured wonderingly.

He met her eyes with a steady stare. "I see you are beginning to understand," he murmured.

And she did. There was no disappointment in the gaze peering at her, no bitterness, or betrayal. Only a desperate hope that he would not lose her, and a love so powerful she almost sank to her knees and wept her relief. This man saw her with all her flaws and adored her despite them.

"I'm sorry. I'll never doubt you again," she whispered, unable to stop the tears, not wanting to stop the hot trails as they washed away the crippling doubt that had held her for too long. "I love you, so much, Oliver."

He kissed her again, and again, and again.

A storm of sensations washed over her senses. His lips moved from hers and began spreading a line of kisses over her jaw and down her neck. She held him to her, feeling safe, loved, the tearing emotions ebbing. They undressed, and he never stopped kissing her. Over her brows, her cheeks, then her lips again, sometimes rough, sometimes tender. She felt lost in a sea of bliss and arousal, a soft gasp escaping Lily as he lowered her to the bed and covered her body with his like a warm, sensual blanket.

"I love you, Lily," he murmured, his lips barely brushing against hers.

She could only stare up at him, lost in the intensity of his gaze. Lily lifted so very slightly and licked along the seam of his mouth. A fleeting smile touched his lips before he ravaged. He wasn't rough. In fact, her love was gentle, yet his touch and every kiss was filled with fiery passion. He trailed his lips down, kissing soft globes of her breasts before licking the hardened tips of her nipples, drawing an eager moan from her throat. Heat raced through her veins and settled into the throbbing heart of her. "Oliver!"

He took his maddening kisses down to her stomach, where he lingered. A lump formed in her throat, and warmth blasted through her. She wasn't frozen with fear at the wonderful and telling caress, only pure need, and she arched her hips in instinctive want. His tongue dipped into her navel, a quick flick before a lingering kiss. She savored the moment, and the love and acceptance he seemed to be communicating with his touch.

He went lower, and teeth nipped along her the insides of her thighs, followed by the tender ministrations of his lips. For a moment, she could barely breathe with wanting him in her, soothing the ache. Then he was there, but with his wicked tongue, which slid through the tender folds of her pussy with erotic precision. She wailed as pleasure knifed through her. He rose, his face heavy with desire, nudged her legs apart, then positioned himself and slid deep into the heart of her.

Oliver loved her with slow, easy strokes, gradually thrusting deeper over and over. Her hips arched, her hands ran down his sweat-slicked back to cup his buttocks, pulling him deeper into the heart of her.

"Without your love, I am incomplete," she gasped tenderly.

A powerful need flared in his eyes, and he bent his head to brush his mouth along her temple then down to her lips, which he claimed in a deep kiss.

It could have been hours later, or a few minutes, but they were locked in a passion that had only room for the love they had for each other. When Lily climaxed, it was a gentle crash but deeply satisfying. With a groan, her love reached his pleasure right after.

Her fingers brushed his face. He pressed his brow against hers for a few seconds before rolling onto his back, taking her with him and tucking her into his side. She yawned, quite indelicately, burrowed into her marquess, and as the comfort of sleep claimed her, Lily knew she could never be happier.

Epilogue

Eight months later...

Lily felt as if she were dying. She was bent over the washbasin in her chamber, heaving. She had been feeling poorly this week, and it seemed the dreadful distemper of the stomach would not ease. Her love shifted her hair, which clung damply to her nape, and pressed a cool cloth against her forehead.

"Do you still want to cast up?" Oliver murmured, his eyes dark with worry.

"No, the feeling has abated, but I do feel tired."

He handed her a glass of water, and she gently rinsed. The maid that had been hovering hurried over and took the washcloth and basin away. Oliver lifted Lily with effortless grace and placed her in the center of their bed. The fire from the hearth blazed, providing much-needed warmth. Still, she shivered and tugged the sheets over her body.

A knock sounded against the door.

"Come."

The door opened, and she almost wept with relief when

her brother-in-law strolled in. His dark brown hair was ruffled, and his kind eyes settled on her. He winked, and Lily smiled. Her sister had fallen in love with David only a few days after meeting him. Lily had thought it improbable, but their love had only grown deeper over the years.

"My lord," he said, dipping into a bow. Then he turned to Lily, a concerned frown pleating his brows.

"May I have a few minutes alone with your marchioness, my lord?"

Oliver glanced at her, and she smiled reassuringly. He left, granting them privacy, but she knew he would not go far.

"How are you feeling, Lily?" David murmured.

"Wretched, just wretched. I have been casting up my accounts three times every day for the past week. My lower back aches, and I feel terribly exhausted most days."

"I'll have you right in no time."

Relaxing at that confident declaration, she allowed him to examine her. If she were the blushing sort, her sensibilities would have been mortified at his thoroughness.

When he finished, David was smiling.

"I am clearly not dying if you are amused."

"This is a smile of pleasure, I assure you."

"What is it?"

"You are with child."

She jolted, a confused rush of emotions tangling through her. "With child!"

His voice droned on, and she only half listened, drowning in a vortex of heartbreaking emotions. "David?"

"Yes, Lily?"

"I need my husband," she gasped out.

"Did you hear what I explained?" he asked gently.

"I did. Would you please get the marquess?"

David left, and a short moment later, Oliver strolled in, his disheveled hair a testament to his worry.

"Hold me," she sobbed.

Her love complied immediately, sitting on the edge of the bed and dragging her to him, burying his face in her hair. "Did David give you a good report?"

"He didn't tell you?" she whispered, fighting the tears that thickened in her throat.

"I confess, I rushed past him the minute he was through the door."

"Oliver…"

He took her mouth with gentle kisses of reassurance. "What is it, my sweet?"

She swiped at the tears that spilled down her cheeks despite her desire to hold them checked. She settled her hands across her stomach, battling the anxiety rising to choke her. "He says…he says I am with child. And I'll be terribly ill and will have to endure early confinement."

Her love froze. "A child?"

"I know…I am afraid to feel such hope. He said the severity of my symptoms indicate I might miscarry."

He gathered her into his arms, one of his hands curving around her neck, fingers working to massage the tension out of her. "I'll not allow it," he vowed.

"You make me feel safe when you hold me." Lily fitted her body more comfortably into his and inhaled his calming scent. "Oliver—"

"No, my sweet. No doubts, no fear. Only joy, thankfulness, and love. We'll do everything that we must, and we'll pray to God to keep our family, but we'll not despair or lose faith. A child is such a miracle, it deserves no negative emotions, wouldn't you agree?"

His assurance crept through her, stealing into her soul, filling it with warmth and love. "You are the miracle," she whispered, her throat and heart tight with emotions.

"You won't say that when I won't allow you to even lift a

book," he said mildly.

He kissed the tip of her nose, the corners of her mouth, before settling on her lips. Lily knew the next several months would be difficult, but she was no wilting flower, and she would do everything that was asked of her and more. "I'll not lose faith," she promised.

"That is all I ask, my sweet. That, and to never stop loving me."

She trailed her fingertips over his face, gently touching every beloved line. "Never."

Then her husband kissed her, holding her close...and nothing else mattered for a very long time.

Dearest Diary,

I've never been so happy or content. I write my final entry, for I believe it is time I put you away. I've written my deepest secrets and hopes within these pages, and my unhappiness and shame have been immortalized. I now wish to end my journey by sharing my greatest happiness with you. I'm the wife of Oliver Carlyle, the Marquess of Ambrose. And only last week gave birth to Caroline Elizabeth Carlyle and Alexander Edward Carlyle.

Cheers,

Lily Carlyle, Marchioness of Ambrose.

Acknowledgments

I thank God every day for loving me with such depth and breadth. Nothing can take his love from me.

To my husband, Du'Sean, you are so damn wonderful. Your feedback and support are invaluable. I could not do this without you.

Thank you to my wonderful friend and critique partner Gina Fisovera. Without you I would be lost!

Thank you to my amazing editor, Alycia Tornetta, for being so patient when I miss my deadlines (which is always) and for being overall a kickass, amazing, wonderful, and super super stupendous editor.

To my wonderful readers, thank you for picking up my book and giving me a chance! Thank you. Special THANK YOU to everyone who leaves a review—bloggers, fans, friends. I have always said reviews to authors are like a pot of gold to leprechauns. Thank you all for adding to my rainbow one review at a time.

About the Author

I am an avid reader of novels with a deep passion for writing. I especially love romance and enjoy writing about people falling in love. I live a lot in the worlds I create, and I actively speak to my characters (out loud). I have a warrior way, "Never give up on my dream." When I am not writing, I spend a copious amount of time drooling over Rick Grimes from The Walking Dead, Lucas Hood from Banshee, watching Japanese Anime, and playing video games with my love— Du'Sean. I also have a horrible weakness for ice cream.

I am always happy to hear from readers and would love for you to connect with me via Website | Facebook | Twitter

To be the first to hear about my new releases, get cover reveals, and excerpts you won't find anywhere else, sign up for my Newsletter.

Happy reading!

Stacy

Also by Stacy Reid...

ACCIDENTALLY COMPROMISING THE DUKE

WICKED IN HIS ARMS

HOW TO MARRY A MARQUESS

THE DUKE'S SHOTGUN WEDDING

THE IRRESISTIBLE MISS PEPPIWELL

SINS OF A DUKE

THE ROYAL CONQUEST

THE EARL IN MY BED

DUCHESS BY DAY, MISTRESS BY NIGHT

If you love erotica, one-click these hot Scorched releases...

PASSION AND INK
a *Sweetest Taboo* novel by Naima Simone

Blackballed from my job. Slinging drinks in a dive bar. The past year has been hell. So when a man who's temptation personified offers me one night with him, I'm all in. But now those unforgettable hours have me facing blackmail from my father: He'll pay for my mom's medical bills, but only if I never again touch the man who has quickly become my obsession. Because the man? My obsession? He's my stepbrother.

WILLFUL DEPRAVITY
a novel by Ingrid Hahn

The Marquess of Ashcroft was born to do two things. Paint and rut. The moment he sees Miss Patience Emery he knows he must have her for both. Patience is a large woman who has resigned herself to having a man only in her dreams. But when Lord Ashcroft approaches her with a chance to act on her bold, scandalous, and depraved desires, she sees her opportunity to indulge in every wicked fantasy she's ever had...

The Last
a novel by Tawna Fenske

Sarah Keating was sure she'd have it all by 30, and there'd be no need to fall back on the marriage pact she made with her best pal from college. But a tipsy message she sends from her birthday party brings Ian Nolan to her door ready to rock her world—and to tie the knot. Their friendship is stronger than ever, and the sexual chemistry is off the charts. But is that enough to make a marriage work, or will one of them fall hard and end up brokenhearted?

Surrender to Sin
a *Fallen* novella by Nicola Davidson

To save her, he must ruin her. Lord Sebastian St. John, dedicated bachelor and a co-owner of the most scandalous pleasure club in London, can't turn the ton's most proper lady away when she begs for his help destroying her reputation. Lady Grace Carrington's fortnight of defiance and self-ruination has to stop the second loveless marriage to an ancient lord her father has arranged for her. But as Grace enters the heady, risky world of an affair with Sebastian, she finds herself inexplicably drawn to him—and she soon realizes two weeks won't be nearly enough.

CPSIA information can be obtained
at www.ICGtesting.com
Printed in the USA
LVHW031519240621
691060LV00003B/135